NORTH OF ORDINARY

NORTH OF ORDINARY

Stories

JOHN ROLFE GARDINER

Bellevue Literary Press
New York

First published in the United States in 2025 by
Bellevue Literary Press, New York

For information, contact:
Bellevue Literary Press
90 Broad Street
Suite 2100
New York, NY 10004
www.blpress.org

A list of publications where certain stories in this collection first appeared is on
page 219 and constitutes an extension of this copyright page.

This is a work of fiction. Characters, organizations, events, and places (even
those that are actual) are either products of the author's imagination or are
used fictitiously.

Library of Congress Cataloging-in-Publication Data
Names: Gardiner, John Rolfe, author.
Title: North of ordinary : stories / John Rolfe Gardiner.
Description: First edition. | New York : Bellevue Literary Press, 2025.
Identifiers: LCCN 2024011888 | ISBN 9781954276321 (paperback ; acid-free
paper) | ISBN 9781954276338 (ebook)
Subjects: LCGFT: Short stories.
Classification: LCC PS3557.A7113 N67 2025 | DDC 813/.54--dc23/
eng/20240419
LC record available at https://lccn.loc.gov/2024011888

Bellevue Literary Press would like to thank all its generous donors—
individuals and foundations—for their support.

 This publication is made possible by the New York State
Council on the Arts with the support of the Office of the
Governor and the New York State Legislature.

This project is supported in part by an award
from the National Endowment for the Arts.

Book design and composition by Mulberry Tree Press, Inc.

Bellevue Literary Press is committed to ecological stewardship in our
book production practices, working to reduce our impact on the natural
environment.

♾ This book is printed on acid-free paper.
Manufactured in the United States of America.
First Edition
1 3 5 7 9 8 6 4 2
paperback ISBN: 978-1-954276-32-1
ebook ISBN: 978-1-954276-33-8

In memory of my sister Helen

With special appreciation for
Wendy Weil,
Frances Kiernan,
and Erika Goldman,
my support, early and late

Wherever you go,
there you are

—Anon.

CONTENTS

INTRODUCTION

By Christopher Benfey

EVER SINCE TURGENEV roamed the Russian outback, returning home with a game bag full of birds and a clutch of literary sketches, location has seemed as crucial to the storyteller's art as to the huckster of real estate. True storytellers—and John Rolfe Gardiner is among our most distinguished, and distinctive, practitioners—have always collected their stories close to home. Whether the roaming is done in Dublin or Yoknapatawpha County, it seems to make little difference as long as the born storyteller knows what to listen for.

In the ten stories of *North of Ordinary*—by turns wistful, quirky, and laugh-out-loud funny—Gardiner does his listening in a pocket of Northern Virginia laced with old villages and new developments, between the nation's capital and the Blue Ridge. In Gardiner's telling, our mounting dependence on privacy-erasing devices facilitates not just listening but outright eavesdropping. In "Familiars," a daughter's running account of her parents' vacation with old friends (and wife swappers) on the Carolina shore is hungrily picked up by the blogger of the "Coffee-Shop Diary" at a neighboring table, "building a small but growing audience for her mother's recycled beach news." The compulsive eavesdropper in "The Man from Trenton" picks a fight with a man on the Amtrak quiet car doing business on his cellphone, with disastrous results for all parties.

Sometimes the listening is more metaphorical, like the aging denizen in the beautiful closing story, "Survival," for whom every house passed on a long walk to the town graveyard has a story to tell. The irony—spoiler alert—is that his own house turns out to harbor stories he's unaware of, touching on the uneasy racial conflicts in the region reaching back to the Civil War. Such not-quite-buried truths are also at the heart of "Virgin Summer," about an eighteen-year-old's awkward summer abroad armed with his schoolboy French ("I'd be very content to be acquainted with the butter") bumping up against Vichy-era sins in a villa in France.

The lost art of building stone walls looms large in "Survival." The man who knows the secrets of the town's architecture happens to be repairing the wall in the cemetery where the town's Black people are buried. "I suppose winter's hard on a wall," the aging visitor says. "Wasn't winter did this," the wall mender replies. Such specialized knowledge—mending walls, mending trees (in the vivid "Tree Men"), signing for the deaf ("Freak Corner"), fixing a lawnmower ("Their Grandfather's Clock")—runs through these stories, just as the same theme was woven into Gardiner's superb collection *The Magellan House*, with its painters and Morse code operators, or the expert enslaved carpenter of his most recent novel, *Newport Rising*.

I'm pretty sure that for Gardiner, himself an expert carpenter married to a master tile maker, such skills have their chief analog in the storyteller's art. The idea that telling stories is closely connected to the specialized knowledge of craftspeople has had a long life. "A great storyteller," wrote the influential German critic Walter Benjamin, "will always be rooted . . . primarily in a milieu of craftsmen." Benjamin believed that storytelling was itself "an artisan form of communication" and that "traces of the storyteller cling to the story the way the handprints of the potter cling to the clay vessel." (Whoever came up with the idea that the illustrations for *North of Ordinary* should all involve hands doing things like tying a cow-hitch knot or signing the twenty-six letters of the alphabet was inspired.)

But the craft on display in these ten stories is above all the master maker of sentences. Some of these are ruefully wise, like this riff on bullies: "How could we know in our adolescent dismay that these would not be the lasting enemies of our lives, that our real trials would be more subtle and born of our own deficiencies, or that the destiny of the Knox boys was already fixed?" And some have an offbeat poetry of their own, like the evocation of "nights tied by rabbit ears to television's big-bosomed Dagmar." If you don't know who Dagmar was, Google her.

And the endings! In the history of the short story, these are always loaded, haunted by the mechanical surprises of O. Henry or Maupassant. Robert Frost, a presence at Amherst College when Gardiner was a student there, once wrote that the successful poem "finds its own name as it goes and discovers the best waiting for it in some final phrase at once wise and sad—the happy-sad blend of the drinking song." Gardiner's art seamlessly elides the ordinary with some higher awareness—one meaning of his title, "North of Ordinary"—and his endings always find ways to be both apt and surprising, though not with some big reversal but a subtler, unexpected one. When those obnox-ious Knox boys drive off with raised middle fingers, the deaf girl, whose achievements with sign language will dwarf their own miserable lives, shakes her head, "not in disgust so much as pity for their impoverished vocabulary." The solitary walker of "Survival" registers a quiet "satisfaction as each abused stone was returned to its natural home."

North of ordinary. Yes, indeed.

NORTH OF ORDINARY

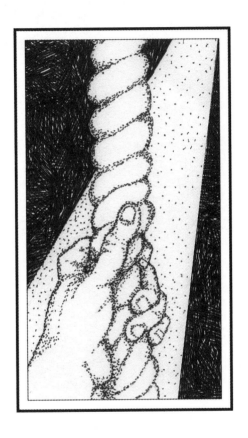

Right off, he taught the boy the cow hitch.

TREE MEN

You're as likely to be hit twice by lightning on a Monday as see a wood chipper pull a man into its maw. Rare, as well, is the member of an arborist crew who hasn't witnessed the horror from the safety of his imagination. Such was I that season, a clinically depressed college boy on medical leave from my nervous scholar's struggle. I took a job with the Walters Tree Service in Winchester, Virginia, hoping outdoor work would be the answer where titrations of the calming pharmacopeia had failed, as if manual labor wasn't host to its own spectrum of anxiety.

My parents, unaware of the depth of my depression, hoped I might study a foreign language in the interim, against a permanent divorce from academia. My girlfriend, whom I supposed found nothing to admire in a man who'd spend a year cutting trees rather than tasting the culture of a European capital, ghosted me before the term became fashionable.

Mr. Walters, who hired me, asked if I was afraid of heights. At my hesitance he told me not to worry. "You won't be climbing, just feeding the chipper. Why do you want this job anyway? Let's see your hands. . . . roll up your sleeves." Only later, I realized that my greatest fears were of things I'd never reached for, and that my girlfriend's estrangement had more to do with the intimacy I hadn't dared than any lack of ambition.

I'd been cutting cordwood for my family's fireplace for years, and passed Mr. Walters's physical with no trouble. It was the college-boy thing and untamed hair that gave him doubts. I said I'd "always been interested in—" "Stop." He threw up his hands. "I don't need a tree hugger. I'm clearing off trouble. I don't care if you know sumac from a locust shoot." I began to explain myself, but he interrupted again. "Where do you live? No drugs? Living at home, are you? Assume you can drive?"

"This is your new man," he told the crew boss, Vernel, whose mouth fell open at the sight of me. "No stranger to hard work," Walters said, pulling this bogus résumé out of the blue.

In fact, I was a complete stranger to physical labor as daily duty. An ordinary middle-class son of America, my exposure to the liberal arts curriculum had taught me my forebears were canny as any in labor-saving devices, starting with slavery, moving on to factory children, then machinery, and a myriad of outdoor machines like Mr. Walters's secondhand chuck-and-duck wood chipper, which lacked safety features.

At the time, his crew was working on private land, taking down dead ash trees. In an open field they needed no preliminary topping. The trunks and larger limbs were being cut for firewood, the smaller fed to the chipper. Right away I was shown how to throw the butt end of branches with force at the noisy machine's mouth, then step back and wait for the lower masticating whine as chips showered into the hopper behind. Nothing but the short entry chute between me and the machine's rolling teeth. If it could chew up a six-inch log, imagine how easily it could digest me.

"Do what he tells you," Walters said, pointing at Vernel, whose shrug made his disapproval clear. In the crew's new pecking order, I'd be pecking last, and I was content with that. It was what I'd wanted, just to be ordered here and there, with months of mental vacation ahead. But there was no clean scrub of the student brain. Outdoor work could not free me from classrooms where I still walked in academic nightmares.

You might ask, If dreams are the work of mad authors and absent editors—fantasies arriving uninvited—why reproduce them here? Because in this early stage of my time among the arborists, unsettling dreams and daydreams were central to the experience. One of them as tormenting in slumber as it was inane on waking. I was protesting a history exam written in ideograph. Bewildered, I was asked by the professor if I'd been absent the day the class learned Chinese.

As academic anxiety gradually gave way to the dangers of my new occupation, there came a particular night of horror when I saw the fingers of a severed hand balanced atop the gate of our wood-chip hopper, as if one of the crew was trying to climb out. Impossible, because I'd just seen him pulled off his feet, arms and head first, surrendering at the same pace as an ash branch to the machine's mechanical appetite. It was turning him into a crimson coloration in the top layer of chips. The crew chief, Vernel, was grinning at me as a dangling foot disappeared. Then I was trying to explain the impossibility of a casket funeral to the man's mother.

THREE OF MY FIVE CREW MATES were authentic wage laborers, I supposed as far into the future as their imaginations carried them; their lives seemed as settled as the brands on their beer cans. What regard should they have for an interloper from a world where thinking was considered work? They never sent me to Home Depot for skyhooks or black-and-white-striped paint, but kept me at a third-person distance while I was no threat to their ranking.

No welcome for me in crew chief Vernel's cold gray eyes set in inward contemplation, promising no hope of brotherhood. He might have been speaking to someone behind him, explaining how far he'd come to sit on his top rung as crew chief. At his direction I kept ice in the water bucket, put the traffic cones out, and at times held a stop sign.

After a month I was still not trusted with a chain saw. I felt no resentment; rather wondered at the contentment of others, at ease with their weekly paychecks and tins of tobacco. There was Ron, who dipped Red Man and hummed through the day, giving rhythm without melody to the day's back-and-forth; Gene, who preferred Skoal, and would flummox me with sexual inference or a question for which there was no self-respecting response: "A good day's work and a piece of pussy'd probably kill him," or "Still using your hand?" If I parried "Get a life," it only begged his question and kept me subject to the crew's amusement.

Then Jefferson, mute until spoken to, the one who might have accepted me as a deserving workmate if I had only paid the full dues of a new man. Vernel was the only one whose soul seemed as calloused as his hands. When we were especially busy, an extra man might be hired from the end of the walking mall, where leftovers of Winchester's wasteland of alcohol and opioid addiction waited each morning, looking for day labor.

The crew kept me aware of my schooling, both how much and how little it meant in their estimation of me. If I'd lived in classrooms all my life, how unlikely I could learn anything from life itself. How useless to know that every action has an equal and opposite reaction if I was going to fall back on my ass the first time I threw a heavy limb at the chipper. I tried not to let some line of poetry or a statesman's quotation betray me, or any showy knowledge that might cause an eye roll or a spurt of tobacco juice.

I've omitted our climber, Carl, from the list—a man apart, who made a remarkable twenty dollars an hour, with the right to hire out on weekends. The climber is the acknowledged hero of a small tree company like Walters's. Working without a bucket truck's perch of relative safety, he may climb on spiked boots a hundred feet or more, with his carabiners and ropes and D-rings to hang over the earthbound in his belted saddle. Swinging by lanyard or high-hung safety line, he hops limb to limb, sometimes tree to tree, an arbor jockey, operating his hip-hung chain saw one-handed, appearing fearless on branches that can scarcely support him.

How fragile his small fame. Not long after I arrived, Carl broke his back, falling in a giant oak. With him hanging limp on a lifesaving branch of the last tree he'd ever climb, we might have thought him unconscious or dead but for an intermittent howl of pain. Gene made a shaky ascent, with Vernel calling up instructions, muttering, "Should have gone up there myself." He was offering instruction for maneuvers already accomplished when Carl was secured in a rope harness and lowered to the ground, where the EMTs were waiting. I was grateful to be one of the earthbound. Not long afterward I was high in the branches of a tree I couldn't remember climbing, falling backward, before I came crashing down on my mattress.

The crew's politics reached scarcely beyond their own welfare. To take gloom off the day of the accident, Mr. Walters had treated us all to lunch at Knosos, the Greek franchise in Winchester. Here I was pushed to the front as the one who would know what spanakopita was. Facing a swarthy man serving behind the counter with a hand wrapped in gauze, I asked what had happened to him.

"Burned," he said.

"Grease?"

"No, Pakistan."

Turning to share my amusement with the others, I saw not a grin among them, only grim nodding at a mutual sense of betrayal by the country's misguided angels of immigration. Not one of them thought the government owed them a thing. No more did I. None ready to accept a favor gracefully, unwilling to be beholden.

Carl got severance; his life in Virginia's green canopy was over. Lost to the crew was his tree-craft, source of their pride and proxy dominion over tall trees. There were thousands of crews like ours across a whole continent of dying ash and other problem trees, crews with their own climbing heroes. But to hear Vernel tell it, one might have thought Carl's leverage from the top of a giant oak could move the planet. I wondered if our little company would survive his loss, while the new fear took its place in my library of dreams. We were all laid off for a week after Carl's fall while Mr. Walters searched the region for his next climber. A scribbled résumé insufficient; Walters wanted to see a new man's skills for himself. He found him working high over an estate by the Potomac River. Hired him right out of a tree at a salary known only to him and Mr. Walters. The man showed up the next week in a rusty truck with his gear thrown in the back. Hitching himself up in his straps, he looked us over, appraising the crew one by one.

His name was Jasper Embry. His red face was pitted, perhaps from smallpox or severe acne. Behind hawkish features his steady gaze revealed nothing. His black hair pulled back in a knot left clear view of a growth on his temple, a dark nickel-size disk. With his narrow jockey's body, shirt buttoned to the neck, and sweat-darkened leather pants, he looked all country without apology.

"I'm from below Grinders," Embry said, "a ways off in the mountains."

One imagined a few bungalows on a blue highway whose only event might be a crossroad, and infrastructure, a speed trap. Walters told us Embry had spent twenty-three years in trees and didn't need a leaf-identification book or bark chart to tell one tree from another. As if to say his work had taught him how to do it, and approaching a tree he did not mean to hug it, but to rid the world of another nuisance.

Embry was already studying his first climb, a double-trunk maple, the larger half split by lightning. Its top branches, brittle by nature, were hanging over a greenhouse.

"You have insurance?" Vernel asked him.

"He'll be my ground man." I stepped back because Embry was pointing at me.

"He just chucks," Vernel told him.

"I'll have him anyway," Embry said, maybe because I was the fresh-faced one, and moving backward as others came forward for preferment. Vernel pointed at Ron.

"No, I'll have him." Our new climber was still pointing at me. There could be no shrinking out of sight. Vernel looked to Walters for support but got none. He may have been in charge of ground men, but Mr. Walters wasn't crossing his new hire. When the boss was gone, Vernel pulled the others aside. They were all looking at me.

From that day forward I was Embry's aide, though still Vernel's minion. First thing, the new climber taught me the cow hitch. He had me tie one around the bottom of a nearby mulberry, setting up the control line that would carry branches safely over the greenhouse. There was snickering as I fumbled through my first lesson.

Walters had been wrong about Embry. He leaned against the maple, feeling its scarred bark in a kind of apologetic salute. On that first day, watching his smooth ascent, his easy movement, branch to branch, my interest in the work woke up. Agile, as if sprung by steel sinew, alert as a squirrel, he rose like an antigravity machine, his feet gripping the bark like the hook side of Velcro. Forgetting my fear momentarily, I imagined myself his pupil.

Somewhere up there, out of sight, a thrush or its winged cousin began to trill and warble, maybe in surprise at human company. Then other birdsong, as if the first had attracted competition. Embry pulled up the chain saw hanging from his belt, gave the starter cord a single tug. A moment later a limb was swinging from a rope, as if a baton was demanding more chirp and trill. I realized it wasn't birds at all. It was Embry himself producing the chorus. From some magic of breath, tongue, and lips, he was making a music of grace-note speed, more like a gift of nature than anything that could be taught or learned.

The branch walking that followed had the weightless appearance of a marionette as he tied off limbs, sawed, and released them to be safely lowered over the greenhouse.

Chain saw, birdsong, chain saw, and birdsong again. Watching and listening, the men below looked up, slack-jawed, ignoring the pile of branches growing beside us. Vernel got out of the truck where he'd been pouting. "Walters ain't paying him to whistle," he said, insulted by the music. He said no one could equal Carl in a tree, and the crew went back to work as Embry flew across to the damaged side of the maple.

Within a week I had mastered our new climber's instruction in several knots—running bowline, alpine butterfly, and Prusik hitch, the loop that holds fast on the middle of a line. Before long I was helping prepare his ropes as he studied the next ascent. Vernel had been watching me as a road-gang guard might a convict testing the range of his shotgun. He made sure I was busy with the two-fingered signal that meant his eyes were on me. When I wasn't helping Embry, I was chucking branches, raking twigs, or on the road, holding the stop sign.

AFTER A FEW WEEKS Embry said, "You can call me Jasper, young fella." A heady promotion. As our bond grew, he hired me to work with him on weekends, beyond the crew's notice. By then he felt free to ask me why I didn't get off my ass and move out of my parents' house. Hadn't finished college yet, I told him.

On an otherwise dismal day, hearing his aviary singing, I could call up to him some line of pastoral poetry, without fear of laughter. "What's it like at that place," he asked me later, "just thinking all day long?"

VERNEL HAD STARTED CALLING Embry "Feathers." I hoped for a counterattack, but none came. The disrespect clear enough, but Embry ignored it. When Walters called me into his office, I knew something was off, and thought he might be getting rid of me. He asked what was going on. He said Vernel had told him I wasn't much account, and what did I have to say for myself. "Did you get off on the wrong foot?"

"There isn't any right foot with him," I said, and was surprised when Walters replied, "Maybe there isn't. If you stay another few months, I'll raise you to eight dollars. Just do what Vernel tells you for now." He wanted to know if the state inspector had been around, and if Vernel was doing side work on the company clock. He was showing me out the door, ignoring my protest at being used as a spy.

I told Walters I'd work another few months if he wanted me, though I'd be ignoring the deadline for readmission to college, passing on scholarship money, and triggering my parents' eviction notice. The truth is, I was more afraid of going back to college—maybe total immolation in that mental furnace—than facing whatever Vernel might have in store. By then I was in full sway of my "country uncle" Jasper Embry and his daily example. I wanted more than his tutoring and tolerance; I wanted his admiration. Not possible while I was content to handle ground ropes, sharpen his chains, and keep his saws topped up with gas and chain oil. Reading my mind, he said, "I could run that fear out of you."

I TOOK TWO ROOMS over an antique store in Winchester's walking mall. A few weeks went by before I dared ask Jasper up to my new quarters for a beer, perhaps a step too far, asking a premature brotherhood. I was more apprehensive than gratified when he said, "Okay, young fella," and showed up a few nights later.

"It's all right," he said, but looking over the bed and chair in the otherwise bare rooms, I knew he meant we should walk out to a bar for our beer. Maybe he thought he'd insulted me, because in the bar he began to share a story beyond my asking.

I'd been wrong about the little community he'd come from. Not three houses on a blue highway—far more remote. A few cabins deep in the West Virginia mountains, farther than you could see across the rolling landscape from the interstate. On a logging road beyond state maintenance. Each home a fortress with a hound on a chain. "Too low in the hollow for rabbit ears to catch the television," they made their own entertainment, he said. Burlap dolls, and a rocking horse from a pallet. They lived what people in the city called the "folk life." He knew this because his father had been taken to Washington one summer, where a fuss was made over his carving and he showed how he fashioned his walking sticks. They had one there in a museum in a glass case.

Think of four families, bound by the necessities of survival but separated by pride of tribe, and two children in forbidden alliance. Thurjean at fifteen in Jasper's arms, defying her father, who had warned Jasper's, "Keep your bastard away from my daughter."

One night she put fireflies in a glass tube and rolled it up in her straw-blond hair. Jasper thought he was "in heaven dancing with an angel." When they were old enough to run over the mountain without getting caught, he carried her off to Winchester, where he started in tree work. Thurjean studied housekeeping on the job, and the science of not having babies. As Jasper's work grew into a career, she managed the money and did the bookkeeping.

"Right away, so happy." A real-life folktale, I thought. The boy with the scarred face and knot on his head whistling up a princess.

"In the stories," Jasper asked me, "don't the trials come first, then the princess?"

As THE SUN FELL, Jasper stared in disgust at a wasted day. We were meant to take out two dead oak trees together, but that Saturday morning was frozen. "If your fingers go numb, you won't know if you cut one off or just mashed it."

We sat in his truck through the middle of the day while it poured icy rain. He knew a man who had worse luck than Carl: "slid out of a sycamore in a rain like this and broke his neck." The wind blew a gale through the afternoon till it was "too late to make a showing." We drove back to the Winchester bar where he'd begun telling his story. Now he wanted mine.

"Where'd it go wrong for you, young fella?"

I explained how a doctor had said my brain got too busy to live with itself.

That can happen to anyone, he said. He knew of a man whose "head got so stuck on one of those twisty blocks, they had to send him to the fifth floor," the locked ward of the Winchester hospital.

"That boy wasn't right," he said, "but look at you."

What did he mean?

"Running backward. Spooked by books. Now you're too scared to climb a tree. Do you want to top out like Vernel? Be ground boss of tree beetles all your life?" Looking up at a climber all day was just teasing my fear, he said.

The next weekend, he said, we had a job in West Virginia; we'd try something different. I guessed what he had in mind. On the way, he could see I was nervous.

"Guess you didn't know I worked way back on a crew with Vernel."

How would I know if he'd never told me?

"A man got struck with a falling branch, and Vernel threw the blame on me. We was both fired. It's no secret. He's told Walters his side of it."

We reached a farm road and Jasper drove across to the fence line, stopping under a tall poplar.

"You've been watching how for months," he said.

If I wasn't frightened before, by the time he'd put me in his spurs and saddle I was shaking like another poplar leaf. Hardly in control of arms and legs as he talked me up to the first low perch. Unrelenting, he told me, hand by hand, how to put slack in the safety lanyard. "Now pick up your feet." I was hanging by the climbing rope. The shaking stopped. When I put a foot down again, I was standing light as an astronaut on the moon, then stepping softly out on the branch and back again.

On the ground once more, I was giddy.

That was a start, he said.

Jasper took me out to the same tree several times in the next weeks, each time coaxing me higher, until I'd reached the canopy with a chain saw hanging from my hip, ready to work in the highest branches. No more involuntary shakes.

With my progress I presumed a full brotherhood, and without invitation I drove out to find Jasper's house where Winchester bumps up against the countryside. The fancier homes to either side of his little place were built on higher ground. The small home looked like a squatter that had defied the bulldozers as "colonials" gathered around to shame it. His gravel drive went down a short incline to an entrance on a gable end. Paint was peeling, glazing all crackled, and the screen door hanging crooked in its jamb.

No greeting but "What are you doing here?"

It took him a while to come to the door, but through the screen I could see a floor plan he might have brought with him from the mountains—kitchen, dining, and bedroom all in one. Bedcovers thrown aside, a scatter of dishes and dirty laundry, and no sign of a princess. Leading me back to my car, he had nothing to say.

Back with the crew the next week, I tried to apologize to him. He waved it off with the back of his hand. "She run off two months ago," he said.

"Thurjean?"

"No, Thurjean was way back." He'd had two women since then. This last one had cleared out overnight, another woman, he explained, who had lost patience with her fate, and then, with a neighbor's assistance, discovered she was a victim of his mental abuse. Before she left, she emptied his bank account. Took the dog, too. She hadn't gotten far, he guessed, because the dog had found its way home again.

Jefferson was first to be fired. The others looked at me balefully. Wasn't I to blame for being there at all? There was a tacit competition after that, all vying to be judged indispensable but unsure whom they were trying to impress, Jasper or Vernel, who thought he was about to be fired himself. That's when he started referring to Jasper as "the gravel-faced bastard" in place of "Feathers." Jasper was still turning his back on the abuse. I supposed his silence might be a gathering storm. I was waiting for thunder.

Walters called me up to say I'd be going back to college soon. If so, he knew more than I did, or maybe it was his way of letting me go. "You may be clever," he said, "but you're ignorant. Working weekends for Jasper, you could both be sued. Tell him I want to talk to him."

"Shouldn't you tell him yourself," I said, waiting to be

fired on the spot. There was an audible breath and a sighing exhale before he said, "His phone's been cut off."

That was a Sunday evening. The crew worked through the next week, ears cocked for the sound of Walters's diesel, lest one of them be caught idling. They were waiting for another shoe to fall. Then another week and they were back to normal, taking turns napping in the truck, thinking trouble must have blown past. But Friday morning I was walking by Vernel with an armful of sumac clippings when he pushed himself into my load. I tripped and fell to the ground. Jasper, from his high perch, came flying down his climbing line to see why all the men were standing over me. Vernel was giving me a hand up, as if nothing had happened.

At quitting time Vernel climbed out of the truck where he'd been dozing. He came over to join the others, showing late-in-the-day solidarity with men who took his orders. We were standing there watching him toss a last locust branch at the chipper. He was still pointing at the roaring machine when his sweater snagged on a thorn and began to unspool in dancing circles from his wrist. As the wool line traveled out, the sleeve was disappearing up to his elbow and beyond, the flying line circling past his bicep, unraveling backward through the order of its knitting. With the denuding of his arm, and the men's yelling lost in the chipper's clamor, eternity collapsed into the moment the line snapped free of his shoulder.

With the motor silenced, Vernel stood there pointing at the defeated machine. Then turned to look at me, posing like a death-defying magician, satisfied his performance had worked to perfection. Jasper was pulling me away, telling me, "That man is dangerous. You can't work here anymore." The others were standing beside Vernel, watching my retreat. I told Jasper I'd already been fired. I'd be coming back Monday for my last paycheck. That I held no grudge against any of them. They had every right to resent me and my disruption, knowing I'd be going back to that place where thinking was considered work.

MONDAY HAD BROKEN GRAY over the farm where the crew waited to say a false farewell to the college boy. Jasper never came down from his high seat in the oak whose dead limbs threatened the house below. He had his own way of saying good-bye. Secure above an ill-natured world, above men whose kindest regard was an admiring envy, above his home over the horizon that could not hold a woman, over the lines of a pitiless phone company, above the boy who proved not worth the trouble he'd spent on his climbing education; still offering grace notes against earthbound disappointment; superior in aerial skill and song. Not one bird and then another, but a medley of trill and warble I hadn't heard before, as if springing unrehearsed from some ancestral habit of questing or contentment, the source maybe a secret from himself. Flying through leaves to his next perch.

Not caring what others thought of me, I raised my uncensored voice to Jasper: "So little cause for caroling of such ecstatic sound, written on the world below, both near and far around." Getting it all wrong, but not what most needed saying: "Some hope whereof he knew, and I was unaware."

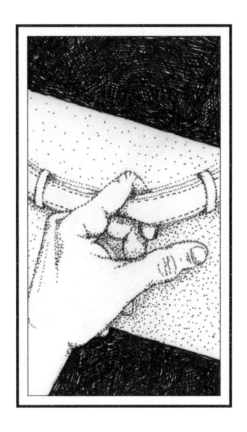

She hooked a finger over his belt and gave a little tug.

NORTH OF ORDINARY

WHEN PETER ASKED, "DO YOU MIND?" Heather only looked down at the empty seat beside her. The men and women of the Freedom College debate team with their faculty adviser, Mr. Abel-Smith, and a dozen supporting students were scattering themselves through the chartered bus in the apparently random way required of young people who do not hold hands or tempt one another with tricks of dress or bare skin (Romans 12:1, 6:13; Ecclesiastes 31). Each stricture at their small college in the Virginia Piedmont could be traced to Scripture.

Peter tossed his head and continued down the aisle.

"Oh, sit," Heather said.

He turned back to join her. A benevolent gesture, he thought, though a little risky, befriending this provocative young soul who hadn't many friends. He only meant to chat with the woman who'd been so candid describing her high school career to his roommate, Jason. There were complaints that the tight-fitting clothes she wrapped on her appealing figure were unfair to men on campus struggling to remain pure till marriage. To Peter she was a puzzle of talent and irritability. He knew she had little patience for the college's practice of mutual correction.

It was already dark, and the chartered bus with

plentiful extra seats and soft, sound-absorbing uphol-
stery offered a sense of privacy that made Peter more
comfortable in her company for the hundred-plus miles
of the return trip up the Shenandoah Valley. There
were students who would correct him for sitting next to
this gifted debater, the one Jason had taken to calling
"Ahab's wife," a not-so-disguised way of calling her a
Jezebel. She was only a sophomore, a little new for campus-
wide notoriety.

Peter had heard talk about the way Heather altered
her outfits, gathering her blouses at the waist for extra
shaping. He gave her a pass on the clothes, but was curious
about her purpose here, where students were being trained
with a Christian imperative for careers in government,
law, and media. When she enrolled, she must have known
that all faculty signed a pledge to teach every subject as an
extension of the Testaments, Old and New. She must have
signed the statement of faith required of all students, one
that said Satan was here on campus, walking among them.

That afternoon Heather had helped the debate team to
victory, defending the proposition "Arctic Penguin, Proof
of Intelligent Design." The topic was announced only when
the teams took the podium. Heather volunteered to lead,
and, without preparation, destroyed her opponent's evolu-
tionist argument with a train of statistical impossibilities
while presuming his familiarity with Bayesian probability
theory. The whispered encouragement of the opponent's
cocksure teammates gave way to groaning as their sure
thing turned to doubt on his tongue. Later, when required
to take the opposite position, she prevailed again, destroy-
ing her own previous position. Afterward, Mr. Abel-Smith

said they could all learn something from Heather—the way she carried the opposition's metaphors to absurd limits while mining her own conceits with caveats against similar attack. To Peter she seemed a bit of a genius.

THE VALLEY'S BEAUTIFUL ALONG HERE," Peter said. "Too bad we can't see it."

They were passing turkey farms, and it was beginning to rain. Sliding rivulets of water on their window were the only visible scenery. She said he'd have to do better than that if he wanted to talk with her. As a senior, Peter was insulted. Other women at the college had told him they liked the way he'd changed over several years from a lean and taciturn Christian soldier into a fleshier, more likable New Testament sort of guy, and this new idea of himself had loosened his tongue. He had to be careful, though. Jason had corrected him more than once for his erratic approach to the other sex, losing his sense of proportion in the excitement of a moment when a lighthearted jest might be taken for hitting on a fellow student.

The blast of an air horn beside the bus startled them. Their driver cursed, changed lanes, and accelerated.

"They're good," Peter said, "the bus drivers."

"Really?"

"It's the truckers' day," he explained. His father was an information officer for the state police, so he knew what he was talking about. On a short-staffed Sunday night like this one, their cruisers disappeared from Interstate 81, leaving the Virginia stretch of the highway to the mercy of the tractor-trailers. Their long, drafting caravans were like trains that would not uncouple, hogging the passing lane, uphill and down. Their speed, which could pass ninety, was governed only by the boost or drag of gravity.

"God's speed? Godspeed to them?"

Subversive cynicism was another trait that ought to be corrected (Galatians 6:1–2). But not by him. Not if there was a chance to draw her out, to get to the bottom of her testy dissatisfaction, or maybe to coax another confession of the way she used to behave in high school.

Mentor, or just perversely curious? He hadn't time to ask a first question before they were thrown against the seat in front of them. A second force pressed him against her, and for a while they were moving north, sideways. Light flashed through the windows left and right, strobing over mouths tight-lipped, then agape. The rotation continued, and Heather was pushed against him. When the bus came to rest at last, it was still foursquare on its tires but facing south in the breakdown lane, a line of trucks blowing by on the right, their drivers unaware of the feat that had taken place in front of them.

A shaken Mr. Abel-Smith offered a piety for their deliverance, and fifteen minutes later they were moving north again, with Peter and Heather rearranged in their seats. Thrown against her in the long skid, he was making amends, establishing with his eyes a modest do-not-cross zone between them. Thinking Heather might have softened in their sudden good fortune of mutual salvation, he suggested an exchange of spiritual histories.

She said she'd rather not.

He persisted. In his case, he said, it was not so much a conversion as a confirmation of things that were already testifying silently in the world around him. "You, know 'only more sure of all I thought was true.' Like that."

If his eyes had not been closed in a moment of inner peace, he'd have seen her pushing a forefinger down her throat, suggesting a productive gagging, before she sank deeper into her seat and said, "Hello?"

Faddish sarcasm, too, deserved correction. Why couldn't they all just speak the truth in common love as the college asked of them? This was referenced in the student manual: Matthew 18:15–17. Instead, she began to question his worldview. "Why do you think they chose that topic for debate? They thought they'd make us look like a bunch of cloacas, that's why."

Did he really think she believed what she'd first argued that afternoon? Did he think laying an egg and balancing it between webbed feet and a warm underbelly to keep it off the Arctic ice till it hatched could be proof of a thoughtful designer? And, by the way, did he think, as one of their professors taught, that more developed animals ran faster to escape the Flood and thus reached higher ground and a more exalted place in the fossil record before they were caught and buried?

Better, he thought, she should keep her voice down. A girl had moved into a seat across the aisle, one row behind them, with an ear wired to one of those little music players. In a community alert to error, he knew this could be cover for eavesdropping. But Heather wouldn't stop.

"What's your major?"

"Government." He was writing his senior thesis on mistaken assumptions about the separation of powers.

"Really? Have they told you where the truth comes from?"

"Deuteronomy seventeen," he said, "fourteen through twenty."

"Do you even know what that says?"

Peter reached for the *vade mecum* King James in his cargo pocket, turned on the overhead light, and began paging forward.

"Don't bother." She turned off the light, closed the little Bible on his moving finger, and offered her own understanding of the passage. "It says when you get to your promised land, choose a king. Not a stranger, but one from your own tribe. And not someone who'll take all the horses and wives and gold for himself. When the king's on his throne, he'll write down the statutes and read them every day, and stick to them."

"And?"

"And? And isn't it a light-year stretch from there to a prescription for the three branches of government? Like looking at a few stars incredibly far apart and tying them together as Orion's belt. Convenient if they actually lined up with one another. Leave it to our chancellor to insist we connect the dots."

"Against Doubt, Vigilance," the college motto, was Peter's default shelter. As others, he was troubled by doctrinal disputes that sometimes floated around the campus. Two of the most respected professors had published an essay in the Christian periodical *Faith Today,* asserting that most of the truth and knowledge on which civilization rests was the gift of irreligious men. "General revelation," they called it. Their contracts weren't being renewed for the next year. Several others were leaving in protest, and some students as well.

"Why are you here?" he asked.

Heather explained how her parents' congregation in Presque Isle, Maine, had raised tuition for one of their young people to go to Freedom College. For her, it was this or stay at home in that bleak far reach of the country. She could have taken courses at the state university, where the motto was "North of Ordinary." Being the brightest thing their little church had to offer, she had come by default, she said, leaving behind the sons and daughters of potato farmers to join the scrubbed-up faithful like Peter from all over the country.

"The brightest, and most in need of . . . correction?" he said.

"People have been talking about me?"

At that moment, with half the trip still ahead of them, Heather seemed to shed her debater's armor, and become a wistful seeker, the woman Peter had hoped to befriend and debrief on the journey home. Her head was bent forward, offering a silhouette in contemplation. She was already violating the no-man's-land he'd arranged for them. With a forefinger at her temple she twisted a dark curl as she began to describe a boy from the potato fields of Aroostook County, the one who had almost derailed her college plan.

She turned to face Peter as she spoke, reaching over to touch his shoulder, giving tactile sincerity to a developing confession. There was nothing very impressive about her, she said, except that she had gigabytes of extra memory, hardly taxed by her education so far. She was challenging Freedom College to overwrite her hard drive with their chapter and verse. They were failing.

A few miles later, her dangling foot brushing against his calf was given a mechanical innocence by an extra vibration of the bus. She said the people she met in the village coffee shop (where else could they gather off campus without some sort of apology?) didn't ask why she'd come to Freedom from a high school in northern Maine. No, they wanted to know why the campus was so eerily barren of people.

It was true. You could drive on the bypass highway next to the college several times a day and not see anyone. Not even a student walking between the several handsome brick buildings. Not a puddle, not a tree, not a soul on the leveled grass plane. To an outsider it seemed not just intimacy discouraged or hidden, but anything that might excite a corrective glance kept safely out of sight. The majority, the ones who weren't taking their secret lives off campus, must have been in their rooms, deep in study.

Yes, she said, it was surprising how much time and intellectual energy were spent parsing inherited truth while ignoring the manifest evidence in the world around them.

"Do you talk this way to everyone?"

She hooked a finger over his belt and gave a little tug, as if to ask for a measure of understanding. Peter thought of changing seats, but there was a story going forward. The Aroostook farm boy's name was Franklin. She'd known him since childhood. She was the one who went for help when he cut his forehead on a barn nail. She moved a finger carefully across Peter's eyebrow, showing where the accident had left a scar, and how close the boy had come to losing his eye.

Franklin, she said, had grown into a big, friendly man-child, a tease-absorbing pal to all, with deep, dark eyes you might mistake for the tools of a penetrating intelligence if you hadn't been sitting in the same classroom and seen him blinking in the panic of an academic challenge. She was justifying advances she made to the hapless schoolmate with the excuse that he actually understood more than he could ever explain.

Franklin looked like a great big country music star, she said. Huge hands, all calloused. Tall, and narrow-waisted, with lots of hair for a country boy. He hadn't a clue about how to respond to her. Much too cautious to touch her. Embarrassed by his clumsiness, he'd have to be invited. Even so, there was some competition for his attention. Most all the girls liked him for refusing to be drawn into the intrigues of the class bullies.

Heather must have known how condescending all this sounded, and how little her apologies could do to excuse the way she'd pushed the helpless Franklin into intimacy. She confessed it seemed banal to her now, not just that she had shed her superiority for him along with her clothes, but how predictably unsatisfactory the episode had been. How unpleasant, in fact. And how tedious all the apologies when she tried to convince him of her remorse. Franklin and his family were members of the same congregation that sent her here. She'd pleaded with him not to confess his seduction to his parents and, for God's sake, not to their pastor.

So, she said, they'd had her family's Jeep while her mother and father were away for the weekend, visiting in

Greenville. She'd driven him out to Echo Lake for the submarine races. And once there, it was as if he was actually watching for periscopes, staring straight ahead at the water, which offered not a ripple. She had to make a game of it—dare, double dare. I'll remove this, you remove that. He wouldn't start. She had to. And not with a barrette or shoelace. Blouse first thing, then her jeans. Franklin was paralyzed until she began to whimper and reprove. How could he leave her at such a disadvantage?

"In a Jeep?"

"You know, in his lap."

Peter didn't know. But he noticed the girl behind them, across the aisle, had removed her earpiece as they reached Winchester. They were turning east toward their Piedmont campus. He began to correct himself for encouraging her to go on, for a curiosity that sullied him by proxy. There was no excuse for the way he'd pried further when she was so clearly finished explaining. By then she was maybe oblivious of his company, busy with herself, cleaning her nails, one by one with a nail of the opposite hand.

Something she'd said begged an explanation, but would anyone else believe he was only probing for the moral of her story when he asked, "What do you think made it unpleasant?"

She snapped up from her grooming and stared at him. She was looking out the window when she finally answered.

"For God's sake! He was clumsy! It was painful!"

She kept her back turned to him, gazing through the window at the rain-freshened night. Finished with him, she turned her scorn to the abuse of the landscape, the backlit windows of a thousand houses, "a measles of development on the fields surrounding Freedom." "Is this Christian habitation? Is this Christian stewardship of the land?"

When the bus reached the college, there was a little crowd waiting for them on the sidewalk. Dr. Edwards, the chancellor, was there, and Mr. Rhoden, vice president for Student Life. Word of the near tragedy had arrived ahead of them. The students had come out of their dorms in pajamas and sweaters. A few held up signs of congratulation for their debate victory. Stepping off the bus, aroused against his better judgment by all the casual touching, Peter reached for something to surprise her. A joke, that's what he intended, something to reverse their positions, turn their conversation upside down and make her laugh.

"So, you want to hook up later?" he asked.

Whether she smirked or actually chuckled, he couldn't tell.

Roommate Jason wanted to hear all about it. "You sat next to her on the way home? Off the map, isn't she?"

"Not that far. Actually, just north of ordinary."

Peter's Monday classes oppressed him. He listened to Dr. Koh, the departing political science professor, defend his distinction between general and special revelation. It was a logical duty to find truth on or off this Christian reservation. A woman left the room, close to tears. Did others wish to leave? Two more walked out. "Good," the professor said, "I'll assume the rest of you agree with me."

Later in the day, Peter's Scripture class held its discussion in the village coffee shop. He was embarrassed by their reading aloud, their confident parsing, their testimonials reaching and overreaching, their affirmations imposed on the tables around them.

He could imagine Heather's scathing review of their sophistry, and even saw himself cheering her on. He was nursing yesterday's adventure—pleasure and bruises. He wanted to see her again, to find a way through her armor, down to the honest, if mistaken, core that drove her candid tongue, to be her full confessor, to share the weight of her past, even if it stained him. Today his sense of worth seemed tied to her, resting on her approval, her friendship, her admiration of his intellect as a peer. He even thought of asking his parents' permission to court Heather.

He was called to the Administration Building by a student messenger in the middle of his afternoon government lecture. Mr. Rhoden was waiting with Peter's dossier open on his desk. Surprised by the half dozen pages in his file, he saw his photo clipped to the top sheet, a thinner self, three years and at least a thousand caramel lattes ago. His old grin, almost as wide as his jaw, a Windsor knot dwarfing his Adam's apple, sport jacket square at the shoulders, hair slicked down, a believer reporting for duty. But ready today to defend to the college dean Heather's wide gift, even if classified as general revelation. He didn't intend to lie for her; neither would he impeach her.

"You know what this is about?"

"The woman from Maine?"

"You don't know her name?"

"Heather . . ." He tried to explain his confused admiration for her. He hoped she wasn't in trouble. He had nothing to say against her.

Mr. Rhoden gathered up Peter's file, as if giving it another chance, but his eyebrows did a doubtful dance, and one by one the pages fell to the desk.

"That's all about me?"

"You have a history of this sort of thing. If you want to stay here, you'll have to apologize. Not just to Heather. To the whole college. Your parents have to be informed."

PETER WENT FIRST THING to Heather's dormitory. Would the girl by the house phone please call her down to the lobby? He waited a half hour. Women passing on their way to the student lounge would not look him in the eye. Eventually one told him he ought to leave. Heather was paged again. Maybe he should come back another time. No, he'd wait. Another reluctant intermediary went upstairs to try. Heather, she said, would not come down. She was afraid to be seen in conversation with him.

Doors along the first-floor hall opened in curiosity, and closed in embarrassment. Maybe, if he sat on the visitors' sofa, it could look as if he was waiting for one of these women to join him for an academic discussion. There was no use pretending that. His pout of injured rectitude was being taken for the face of a penitent. He supposed his nervous innocence, if read by a lie detector, would send the recording pen into guilty oscillation. Still reluctant to leave, he begged a wary freshman to deliver a note: "What did you tell the dean?"

Heather sent a quick response in block capitals. "THE DEAN CALLED ME IN. HE SAID I SHOULD WATCH OUT, AND THAT YOU HAVE A HABIT OF THIS."

Peter phoned home to head off the dean's call, but it was too late. No, he told his parents, he hadn't harassed the woman. "Hooking up doesn't have to mean that. It was a joke. She knew it was a joke."

His father wasn't so easily put off. "You meant actually hooking up, but it was a joke? Or did you mean why don't we talk later, and it was innocent and didn't have to be a joke?"

"You're confusing me. They won't even tell me who reported this stuff."

In the week that followed, he had only occasional glimpses of Heather in the cafeteria. With a remade reputation as a victim, she was gathering new friends, who positioned themselves on either side and across from her in the cafeteria, or while she sat vulnerable in any public place, their baleful glances warning Peter to keep his distance. He'd been removed from the debate team and barred from extracurricular activity while the case against him was prepared for the student judiciary.

Peter didn't care what Rhoden thought. Rhoden was an ass. Whatever was in Peter's files, no accusers had made themselves known to him, and there could be no action against him based on hearsay. If Heather had allowed this storm to blow up, he doubted she would ever testify against him. But he gathered she'd been all innocence in front of the dean. She'd said she thought Peter must have been joking. He took comfort in knowing that she wouldn't speak against him, but he wanted more than that. He was still angling for her kind regard. After a week had passed, he asked another girl on the debate team to find out how things stood between Heather and him. Her report was strangely unfriendly: "The boy's lost his voice, and sends a carrier pigeon?"

With more time to reflect, his parents took Peter's side, counter-attacking with a letter to the dean, citing slander—"He has a history of this sort of thing"—passed from Rhoden to Heather, and circulated among the students, defaming their son among his peers. Besides, they argued, the original report of harassment hadn't come from the girl herself, but had been made by a third party, and passed to a fourth, then a fifth, before it reached the dean. Peter had a copy of the letter with his father's comments for him in the margin:

"No wonder that place can't get accreditation."

"Why don't you come home. We'll demand a tuition refund."

There was only a semester left before his graduation, and Peter was holding out for his degree in government. With the legal leverage identified by his father, he should be able to force the college to let him walk with his class. In the meantime, they couldn't make him apologize. While the chancellor and his rebelling professors argued over the moral authority of Saint Augustine, Peter shared his situation with Jason, whose reference to Saint Matthew—rain would fall on the just and the unjust—was little comfort.

On his way to dinner one evening, Peter found a note hanging from the slot in his mailbox: "Waiting for you at Rock Faith in the Rapture Room. Call yourself 'The Tongue.'" It was signed "Candy Cane."

He tore the note to pieces and tossed the dirty confetti in a trash bin.

HE KNEW WHEN TO ENTER the cafeteria, the quarter hour after six, when Heather would already be seated in the farthest corner of the room at a table unofficially reserved for members of Eden's Fruit, the college maskers and their techies. This clique, too, had been attracted to Heather, hoping their sympathy would lure the talented, abused girl into the drama club in time for the spring Passion. A step up for her, Peter mused, from Jezebel to Magdalene—if that's what they had in mind for her. She seemed to be doing most of the talking, provoking laughter, making theirs the loudest corner in the room, paying no attention to his lonely meal.

HE USUALLY FINISHED STUDYING around midnight, and unwound with a solitary walk around the perimeter of the campus. It was a rectangular stroll bounded by the bypass highway, two country roads, and a Christmas tree farm, which, in the brief history of the college, was known as the hiding place of illicit affairs, the trysting ground of a romance between two star students discovered locked together on a bed of pine needles, fallen from grace and summarily expelled. But now married and prospering, moving up in Christian-influenced governance.

Peter, who passed the artificial forest on most nights, had heard laughter from deep in the lines of spruce trees. He carried a flashlight but was reluctant to point it at happy noises, though he'd taken the entrance oath to shine a light wherever Satan might be found in his college.

The end of his walk took him back across the center of the campus, past the two women's dormitories and under

Heather's room, where he was now in the habit of looking up for the silent news from her window. Open or closed? Heather's air fresh that night or conditioned? Lights on or off? Was she awake behind the curtains, or tucked away in bed?

PETER'S FINAL SEMESTER DRAGGED ON with Heather always a step out of reach or turning away before he could beg a word with her. She did appear in the spring Passion, not in the role of Magdalene as he'd imagined her, but cross-dressed as Thomas, darkened with charcoal, made up to have the doubting apostle appear more sinister than Judas. He saw her, too, in another debate, her eyes dancing past her opponent, capturing the hall while first annihilating an odious phantom called "the unitary power of the executive" as a creation of megalomaniacs mad with Potomac Fever, then resurrecting it as the intention of three Founding Fathers, with references to the Federalist Papers.

In the week before graduation, Jason went home to Maryland to study. Peter, with no one in the room to correct him, used his freedom aggressively. On the way back from his midnight walk he called up to the open, fully lit window, "Heather!"

She came to the window in a loose shift, hugging herself. But seeing him below, she threw her arms theatrically wide, draped a half-covered bosom over the sill, and called down, "Is it peace, Peter?"

Confused, he had no answer.

She laughed, closed the sash, and pulled down the

shade. Her lights went off, and so did others, until the whole dormitory loomed dark and accusing over him.

"Is it peace?" He'd heard this before but couldn't place it.

Back in his room, he opened his Concordance and found the words in 2 Kings with the answer. "What peace so long as the whoredoms of thy mother Jezebel and her witchcrafts are so many?" And further on, the same question was asked by Jezebel herself before she was thrown from her window and eaten by dogs.

He couldn't sleep on that. Nor had mutilation destroyed the message he'd found in his mailbox. Without Jason watching over his shoulder, he was free to roam cyberspace, maybe risk his hard drive to the nasty kind of attack that would linger in its memory, even if lured only once to a dangerous place.

He had no trouble reaching the Rock Faith site, where he knew other Freedom students had found the solace of righteous company. He could argue that it was his duty to expose whoever would defile that refuge. Clicking on the Rapture Room, he was further reassured by a screen promising privacy in a "personal corner," where he was offered a final chance to turn back, to cancel or continue. Choosing "Continue," he watched the forefinger of his right hand type the name she'd given herself, and then more slowly, the name she'd given him.

His father had been right. The college had abused him. He could say he only persevered against the defaming accusations to earn the degree it owed him, so that his years there would not have been completely wasted by an overzealous dean or a rash decision of his own. By comparison with the last month, his whole career at Freedom seemed of little significance. Nothing of moment as long as Heather, whom he admired beyond reason and in defiance of his professed faith, refused him the courtesy of a simple conversation, her confession of his innocence, even a sign of regret.

His signal brought the receiving computer to life. His respondent was awake and typing.

"I thought you'd forgotten me. Are you ready to play?"

"No."

"You're no fun."

"Who are you?"

"Do you know what Professor Koh calls government majors? He calls them 'the chancellor's eunuchs.' What are you wearing?"

"Who are you?"

"As if you didn't know. Wait a minute. . . . There, that's better. I was too hot."

"It's the middle of the night. I must have woken you."

"So, imagine me now."

"I won't imagine anything."

"No. I don't suppose you will. Why did you wake me up?"

"I want to talk about Jezebel. I never called you that."

"Look. Do you want to be stupid all your life? Don't you see what's happening here? The best people are leaving. Anyone with a mind of their own is asked to check their intellect at the door."

"What if I print this and take it to the dean?"

"The correspondence of Candy Cane and the Tongue? I don't think so."

HEATHER WAS GATHERING MORE ATTENTION as a martyr to Peter's effrontery. In the last week of the term, he was called to answer the testimony of two more women, unnamed, who accused him of stalking the sophomore from Maine, harassing her at night from the sidewalk under her window. Near the top of her class, she'd never lost a debate. To her following of sympathizers, she had come to Freedom for protection from a predatory world, from a high school where she'd been attacked by a big, tricky farm boy named Franklin, and was looking now for sanctuary in a community of truth and humility.

The graduation tent beside the highway looked like the pointed drum of shiny plastic you'd see over a modern mini circus. Under the tent, Peter was walking with his class. He wondered if the scroll they'd present him would be blank, or deficient in some official way. Even with his diploma in hand he was wary, searching it for the placement of a Latin negative, *non est*, or something like that.

The night after graduation he stayed on in the dorm to confront Heather once more, even if just in the ether. Not to renounce duplicity so much as to marvel at the Trojan horse on which she'd jumped the college gate, the ease at which she'd grazed among the faithful. She gave no quarter, but congratulated him as one of the chancellor's freshly papered Christians before the Rapture Room went dark.

She did the finger alphabet, a *to* z *in twenty seconds.*

FREAK CORNER

The new Margaret Kipps made her switch without going under the knife. This in mid-twentieth century, when an operation for the full change might have been offered in Scandinavia, but not to Alfie Kipps of Arlington, Virginia, who became Margaret in dress and address in the summer of 1953. No loss or gain of genitalia.

I don't remember how that detail was brought to light, whether by my parents' investigations or the reports of shaken neighbors in the Meadow Brook development. We could only imagine the inward clap that must have concussed his household before outward reverberation shook our community to its farthest reaches, where a maiden sister in a surviving Victorian would lower her voice to begin, "My dear!"

Alfie, in his late twenties, still living at home, had been working, he told us, in the city, in the circulation office of a trade magazine as a punch-card operator, that once pervasive data-management job, long extinct. The change was more shocking because Alfie had never shown us a feminine inclination. In fact, there were young women who used to drive into our development to wave at the Kippses' porch, coming and going. We assumed it was a mark of Alfie's popularity, not a sign of social reticence or sexual confusion.

Now Alfie—Margaret, please—began to follow the era's fashion of soft wool sweaters, presumably padded, and skirts that fell demurely to just above her ankles. My parents' reaction was pity: "Poor boy." My concern for him was mixed with skepticism at such a sudden transformation. Memory says he affected a brunette wig of hair that fell to his shoulders until his own should catch up to its dutiful length. His voice seemed stretched to a higher note, something he might be trying on, like the new clothes.

My mother asked me to ignore the changes. As if it were a social duty to accept the remarkable alteration, even as she and my father discussed the "situation" across the street. Meanwhile, Meadow Brook at large was not opening its arms to our newcomer. Small children were warned away, teens felt predictably threatened in their emerging sexuality, and adults were troubled by the notoriety coming our way.

Gregory and Harmon Knox, who lived a few doors away from us, members of my senior high class, were openly hostile to Margaret. They made sure we were all aware of their disgust. Gregory, a year older than Harmon, had gotten himself held back in junior high—I think to become his brother's closer ally in life's progression, making a disruptive team in our shared classroom. They existed, it seemed, to threaten Meadow Brook and our schoolyard with their black hair in duck's ass dos fixed in place with Vitalis, that grease and alcohol preparation, since gone the way of the punch cards.

Enabled in arrogance by a proud father, the brothers drove a Chevrolet heap with ear-blasting glass-pack mufflers. The rest of us, standing mute at our school bus corner, waited in impotent irritation for the daily insult of their racket, and their obscene gestures, sometimes a vileness directed my way: "Has your retard sister's thing got hair on it yet?"

How could we know in our adolescent dismay that these would not be the lasting enemies of our lives, that our real trials would be more subtle and born of our own deficiencies, or that the destiny of the Knox boys was already fixed? No match for the provost marshal in the brig at Fort Dix, New Jersey, where they eventually spent the second year of army tours before dishonorable discharges and lives beyond our ken on some other unlucky street.

"Freak Corner" was the brothers' name for the end of the block where our brick rambler stood across from Alfie Kipps's house, identical but for some glass-brick courses in the front wall, too cloudy to see anything but shadows moving behind them. Our house, the other piece of their Freak Corner, being home to my sister, Gayle, whose limited vocabulary and floating inflections left a constant question on her face: Is this the way it should sound?

Gayle, prelingually deaf, never heard a word our parents said, though it took them nearly two years to understand that placing herself in front of them when they spoke was not a child's remarkable politeness, but her need to see the movement of their lips. Accepting the diagnosis, they were determined, with little debate, that Gayle would be an "oralist," a mainstreamed member of the hearing world.

Her early years must have been a time of dim confusion and bewildered anxiety. As she grew older, the indignities were felt if not heard: "Call her 'dummy.' She can't hear you." Worse came later—subjection to the world's pique at what it took to be her conceited diffidence, then to pity for her presumed cognitive deficit. I grieved with Gayle, which only gave fuel to her frustration.

RETARD? I HADN'T THE READY WIT to counter the Knoxes' uninformed cruelty. I was too angry to be afraid of them but couldn't offer a reasoned defense of my sister's quavering voice and pleading eyes, the contortions of her mouth, the disturbing approximate sounds of speech. She was quite beautiful when her face was relaxed in its normal symmetries.

But what was retarded if not a daily ride to special classes in a bus with the handicap symbol announced on its back door, hours spent with a remedial teacher, and a speaking vocabulary at age ten of perhaps a hundred words? I loved her and accepted that her deafness must be loved as well. She turned fourteen in the summer of 1953. I was almost seventeen, a rising senior, her regular chaperone and protector.

I shouldn't say our street was ruled by bullies. Nor was it some benighted middle-American cul-de-sac spending its days in ignorant goodwill and nights tied by rabbit ears to television's big-bosomed Dagmar. Across the way, Mr. Kipps, Margaret's father, was an officer of the region's electric company. Other near neighbors—a real estate agent, a high school principal, a clerk in the Government Printing Office, a pharmacist, a stockbroker, a title attorney, the manager of a vacuum cleaner store—were men and the occasional woman who had achieved comfortable middle-class lives.

The Knox boys' father was a bail bondsman, with an office next to the county courthouse. My father was manager of men's clothing at Woodward & Lothrop, that staid Washington department store where you could still check the fit of new shoes through a fluoroscope, see your skeletal toes squirming in a sea of electric green.

When TV antennas began to alter Meadow Brook's roofscape, radio was still our home's prime medium. The radio, once a humming of vacuum tubes nesting in oversized living room furniture, had shrunk to fit in streamlined bedside plastic. It might seem a transparent feint at authenticity to seed my sister's story with yet another of that decade's commercial markers, but her story was no fiction. And to the brother of deafness, radio, as nothing else, signified her missing American childhood—comedians, singers, and serial heroes.

This was long before signing for the deaf became a duty at public events. The words *rock* and *roll* had not been twinned as musical genre, so no band called Lather, Rinse, Repeat. Still in the atom's tomb, punk and rock had not combined, so that musicians still unborn had not thought of Laudable Pus as a name that would travel so well from Brighton to Blackpool and across the Atlantic.

When the pioneering Christine Jorgensen went under the knife to become a woman, the shocking story did not fly the ocean in an internet instant, but reached us a week or so later on the cover of *Life* magazine. Who but the bravest would dare such extreme deviation in that decade when *commie* and *queer* were thrown so carelessly at the least aberration? To us it might have seemed Alfie had turned into a woman so that the distant Christine wouldn't be so lonely and despised in the world's eyes.

It shouldn't have surprised me in that time when so few of us knew how insidious and ripe were our own prejudices that my sister, Gayle, would be the one most intrigued by Alfie's transformation, the least threatened, the most eager to seek his company, our family's goodwill ambassador. With a fortitude we lacked, she crossed the street to wait on the Kippses' stoop each afternoon for Margaret to come out and sit beside her.

From our house I could see Gayle entertaining her new friend with hand signals—I supposed of her own devising—until my mother would send me across the street to fetch her home for supper. That was Gayle's only homework. We thought of it as a daily good deed, a window scene that could wet our cheeks. I watched beside my mother as sentiment, at first, overcame our fears for my sister.

In the fall of her thirteenth year, she'd begun to move with a lighter step, and her face was lit with a new enthusiasm. In her mumbling way, Gayle was attempting words we could not make out because it didn't seem possible she could know them, even abstract ideas—reason, eternity. For some time, her speech had been left behind her reading level.

Her handicap had disguised a phenomenal intelligence, far beyond the norm of her hearing peers, and the polar opposite of the impression she made in our neighborhood, where she was presumed to be an empty vessel, a Sphinx without a secret. But now a miracle to her teachers for a child in her predicament. By rights, she might have had the vocabulary of a pre-kindergartener by then, and commensurate developmental delay.

For a time, our parents' pride in their prodigy pushed aside questions of what lay behind the transformation. There was Gayle, grinning at a Salinger story in a magazine beyond my interest or comprehension. Had it all been unwitting trickery? Had she actually been hearing words and processing grammar while barred from response by some neurological anomaly? Was she a mute we were forcing to speak?

From age seven, she had a private tutor, Aimee Chapin, fresh from postgraduate audio study and a charming presence in our lives. Shy, with a saintly devotion, Aimee had been hired to make Gayle a speaking member of the hearing world. Nothing less—or more—period, a firm command. Aimee sat beside Gayle in school, and spent hours alone with her in our home, with endless patience for her deaf charge.

How clever Aimee was in her grand deception of my parents. How stealthy, using me as intermediary to cover her betrayal of their no-signing order. Sometimes when she left the house, she would pull me outside with her to chat about Gayle's progress. One evening she stopped beyond our front door, her eyes pleading for understanding, her face so close to mine, I thought she might be waiting for me to take her in my arms.

"Your sister *is* a freak," she said, "an intellectual phenomenon. Were you aware that people can have ideas before they have the words to express them?" If she was walking here on the edge of philosophical debate, so, it seemed, was her student. "Do you know what Gayle asked me this afternoon? 'Is eternity on both sides of us?' Where do you think that came from?"

Aimee knew a family struggle lay ahead of us, and she wanted me in Gayle's corner when the battle began. And my sister, breaking through chains of ignorance, though well aware of Aimee's danger, could not withhold the truth any longer. Her grand transformation had been thanks to Aimee's instruction, in total disregard of our parents' commands.

"Columbia Institution," Gayle wrote on a scrap of paper, a preparation for my own tutorial. Next time Aimee had me alone, she held nothing back. Did I know that if I could not name things, I'd remain a stranger in the world, even in my own home? Did I know the native deaf, if taught speech alone, were lucky to speak at fourth-grade level when they left high school, that this could have been Gayle's fate? Had I noticed that my remarkable sister now had a grammar and critical mass of vocabulary that was growing in all directions as a context of visual symbols began to teach her what she could not hear and scarcely pronounce? That she had a phenomenal plasticity of mind that might one day study elusive dimensions of mathematics if that was her passion? It wasn't. Though letters stumped her lips and tongue, they were already flying through her mind in connected patterns that a hearing child might envy.

In short, did I know what had happened?

By then, perhaps I did, but I didn't want to admit it. For almost two years Aimee had been teaching Gayle sign language, flouting our parents' edict, and Gayle, knowing she was in danger of losing her confidante, her treasured Aimee, had kept it a secret between them. Signing—anathema— that pit of grimacing pantomime my parents could not bear to have their daughter fall into. Gayle, Aimee lectured me, should not be held in a conceptual prison, even if with the best intentions. There was a world of joyous communion waiting for her. In fact, she said, my sister had come too far for any of us to prevent it.

Aimee had no right to solicit my part in her work with my sister. It was unprofessional, unethical. At the time, I had to side with my parents in this, but their firing Aimee, their effort to have her barred from all deaf instruction, brought a swift reaction in the house—locked doors, sobbing, a shelf of old stuffed animals with legs removed. The tantrum was not infantile meltdown, but forerunner to Gayle's passive-aggressive attack, her refusal to speak at all, turning away from the movement of our lips.

Yet every afternoon she walked out of the house, across the street to join Margaret Kipps on her stoop, where, from our living room window, we could witness another performance—arms, hands, plying the air, head cocked inquisitively from side to side. It was tormenting to know that neighbors would be taking this for chaotic neurological disorder, or imagining her a lesser organism stirred only by the satisfaction of instinctive needs. Not Margaret. If she was baffled, she responded with complete absorption and hand-clapping admiration.

Gayle was showing us all a latent animation, stifled so long, now free to stab not just at the names of things—smells, tastes, sensations—but her emotional appreciation of the whole perceived world. And as Aimee predicted, her radical whirl of symbols was ready to become a feast of sharing, regardless of our fears or any efforts to restrain her.

IF GAYLE WAS AN EMOTIONAL MESS after Aimee's firing, my parents wept in private. I was the dry-eyed pivot they swung on, or grabbed at for support. Not a good time for them to be reading the conventional texts on deafness: "Signing foments the passions, while speech elevates the mind." This, along with "Signing feminizes the male and makes the female masculine," while our brave Gayle crossed the street each afternoon to visit her ambiguous "sister." These warnings were uppermost in my mother's mind. And there was Gayle, teaching the sign for *transvestite*, a loose-wristed twist of the hand in front of her chest for the admiring Margaret, who reached for the hand in gratitude.

I was glad the Knox brothers were not out on queer patrol. I've tried to think of something that would redeem those two from stock players as one-dimensional fools in Gayle's history. But I could as easily convince myself that nature had a purpose for two more wasps. Nothing to admire—only their likeness to a Biblical plague, testing our faith, or teaching us to appreciate decency by showing us the opposite.

Another afternoon when I crossed the street to bring her home, Gayle was sitting with Margaret on the front steps, a hand on her knee, as if her friend needed comforting. Annoyed by the familiarity, I sat down beside them to coax my sister home. I was met with a twist of her shoulder and head turned away. At that moment the Knox boys came around the corner in their noisy heap. Seeing us, they braked suddenly and rolled down their windows.

"Freaks!"

"Fairy!"

"Queer bait!" was their sign-off as they gunned away.

Margaret stiffened. "I'd chase the bastards if it wasn't for this damned skirt." Remembering who she was, she softened and asked, "Do you like my new outfit? Garfinkel's ladies' department."

If Gayle had missed Margaret's actual distaste for women's clothes so tastefully purchased, she could not have missed the change of mood that had just occurred. The same day, our mother had learned more about Margaret, something heard at market. Her parents were moving to their retirement in South Carolina. She'd be living alone. "And she isn't a transsexual; she's a transvestite, and a woman in spirit."

Both unfamiliar words to us. No matter their definitions, I knew something was twisted. But Gayle was far too invested to find fault in Margaret's sisterhood. She had her own dilemma—our parents' loving intention pitted against her struggle for freedom. Persistent in turning her head away from every movement of their lips, she was slowly forcing them to relent, undeterred in her resolve to be part of a signing community.

TWICE A WEEK I DROVE HER to the Columbia Institution campus in Washington. Then it was every day. A revelation. Gayle and I reintroducing ourselves in a way that made us happier in each other's company. My signing proficiency would never catch up with hers, but this whole-self language left the hearing world somewhere outside our reborn mutual love.

She and a dozen other teenagers were transformed that summer into a brother- and sisterhood of hand actors in a

drama of laughter with the relaxed brows of dawning comprehension. Not in the Columbia classrooms, but in the
cafeteria and other gathering places where two older students were introducing them to the full informal signing
system of their peers, what is now called American Sign
Language, along with the hand alphabet, already fixed in
Gayle's muscle memory. She was timed at twenty seconds,
a to *z*. I watched her hands rising, swooping, pointing, in
feints too fast for me, then a sudden switch to letters with
her fingers in prestidigital dazzle. The muscles of her face
shifting in shades of pleasure, in harmony with her hands'
performance.

Gayle captivated those peers, her physical beauty only
half the attraction. She was always in front of someone,
ready to inform or be informed. At the end of the informal
classes one of the mentors took the group under the shade
of the "swearing tree," a live oak, where he led a rump tutorial in cursing, a wide-ranging hand-and-finger medley of
street vulgarity. The young initiates were freed once over,
arming themselves with a code of theatrical defiance, and
Gayle absorbed the whole of it. Though, as one of her newly
discovered authors had written, there could be no final
glossary of words whose intentions were fugitive, especially
not in the expanding world of signing. The shared mischief
was a further liberation.

For all that, Gayle came home each day to Freak Corner, to a community with little comprehension of her new
world, to neighbors who still patronized and pitied, and to
her own fearful parents, forewarned by the oralists of the
perverse dangers in signing. My father was not so worried
that Gayle might acquire masculine traits but was prey to

any father's fear of a daughter's new alertness to the ubiquity of sex in the world. He thought the signing made her look cheap. Freakish, if he'd dared to say the word.

I supposed the fired Aimee's intentions must have been the same as the Columbia Institution's: a struggle for the acceptance of signing against the ruling orthodoxy of deaf education—oralism. Not so. Columbia had been warned about Aimee. She was barred from their campus. They were not ready to accept that signing could be a fully legitimate language, unaware that change was afoot. A new member of the faculty, a man name Stokoe, who had come to teach Chaucer, was about to rile the community with his assertion that signing, dismissed by some as "picture writing in the air," was actually a complete language, with a grammar beyond shapes and gesture, hidden in the fourth dimension of timing.

The Knox brothers had been stalking Margaret Kipps, following her in their car into the District. They brought back a story for Meadow Brook. There was a nightclub in the city's southeast where men who dressed as women looked for friendships. The brothers had seen Margaret give a doorman money before disappearing inside. Another time, they had followed her to work, not into Washington as she'd said, but somewhere on the Virginia side of the Potomac, where her car disappeared down a restricted roadway.

Alarmed, Mother told Gayle she'd have to give up

visiting Margaret or else forfeit her lessons at Columbia Institution. Gayle pulled me to her room and declared, part pantomime, part in writing, that she wasn't giving up her friendship with Margaret, who'd been eager to learn signs herself; nor would she be kept from Columbia. Was I on her side, or not?

She told me the new professor had chosen her for a demonstration that would prove what he'd been saying, that signing was a full language. She circled her palms over the tips of her still growing breasts—I'm excited—and we shared a grin, at our parent's expense.

"But what about—" My hands moved over my own chest, down my sides, and over my hips, signifying *dress*, meaning, What about Margaret?

Gayle didn't care how Margaret dressed or what her clothes signified. She was defying our mother, walking out of the house that very afternoon, crossing the street to see her friend again. She knew we'd have a curtain pulled aside, watching her every move. Margaret opened the door but didn't come out to sit with Gayle on the stoop. Instead, the two of them disappeared into the house.

Mother started for the front door, then turned back for the telephone. To call my father? The police? But what would she say? My daughter is visiting our neighbor, who wears women's clothes?

"Give them a few minutes," I begged her.

A few minutes became five. There was no holding Mother back. We crossed the street together and knocked on the front door. Two of our neighbors were watching from their stoops as we pushed through the unlocked door.

"Gayle! Gayle!" my mother called through an empty

hallway, as if fear for her daughter could restore her hearing. We went searching through rooms, upstairs and down, before we saw the two of them facing each other in the backyard, playing a simple game of pat-a-cake, their hands never even touching. Actually, another signing lesson under a dogwood tree.

"Gayle was teaching me how to say *charade*," Margaret told us before asking Mother, "Have you come to rescue me?"

Toward the end of summer came the defrocking. Margaret was Alfie again! Rushing across the street to us in a T-shirt and trousers now, bosom gone, in full throat as Alfie Kipps. "What happened here today?" he asked, turning first to Gayle, as if she'd betrayed him. There was no explanation for the masculine renewal.

Someone had broken into his house, ransacked rooms, emptied drawers, rifled the closets. There was broken glass and china on his kitchen floor, and a lipsticked message on the wall too foul for repetition. Well, then, had any of us seen the Knox boys entering his house? We must have seen something.

Gayle was close to tears as she watched him drive away, thinking he was renouncing their friendship for good, never mind that he'd deceived all of us—not a woman in any sense, it seemed. Gayle was thinking she might never see him again. I walked across the way for a look through his windows. Over the kitchen counter was the lipstick message on the tile and a crude phallus flying toward the sink.

That evening there were police cars in the street, officers

at the Knoxes' door, and more county police the next afternoon, with warrants this time, pushing past Mrs. Knox. Later we saw the brothers come out their door to show the departing police cruisers their one-finger salute.

No LIGHTS THAT NIGHT in the Kippses' house; Alfie hadn't come home. Later in the week, still no trace of him. Dark sedans with tinted windows parked in front of his house, a federal posse there for a closer look at the vandalized residence. Alfie was gone. Gayle's hands flopped over, palms down, as she gave a shrug for a question mark. Was he dead? she was asking. Out of our mother's sight, she confessed to me she'd known for some time that Alfie's emergence as Margaret had not been the transformation he'd pretended. He was frightened, she said. His makeup had become sloppy, black stubble showing through a moist layer of white powder.

GAYLE DIDN'T TELL ME what to expect at Columbia, which had recently changed its name to Gallaudet. She wasn't sure herself. We had just gotten out of our car on the campus, and were met by a dean. "Professor Stokoe's demonstration isn't going to happen," he told me. But why tell me instead of her?

Because he doesn't know how to sign, Gayle explained. Students gathered around my celebrated sister, begging her to stay. She got back in the car and made me drive her home. She wouldn't jeopardize her chance of enrollment there.

Turning into Meadow Brook, we saw Gregory Knox

wantonly banging his push mower into the curbstone at the edge of his lawn. He stopped long enough to call out, "Where's your fairy?" Not chastened by the police investigation, more likely embarrassed to have his house searched for evidence he'd been with his brother on a panty raid in the Kippses' place.

That week the evening paper carried the story of a police search for a missing man, Alfred Kipps of Arlington's Meadow Brook development, lately employed by *Broadcasting*, a trade magazine with offices in the city. The morning news brought another report of the disappearance, with a denial by the magazine that Mr. Kipps had ever been employed there. His story stayed news with the revelation that Kipps was a transvestite, leading another group of reporters to our street. We told them we were as mystified as our neighbors.

Weeks, months, a full year with no word of him before journalists were back on the missing man's trail. Alfred Kipps (was that even his real name?) had been an employee of the Central Intelligence Agency, a "Company man," far off the Company's reservation, spying on an American citizen, they reported—and not just any citizen. This was political tinder.

Meanwhile, Gayle had been accepted at Gallaudet, and I had enrolled at Georgetown University across town, my signing proficiency jumping ahead with every vacation we spent together. We spent a lot of time on old wounds. Gayle had never believed Alfie was dead for a palms-down certainty. I asked her if she missed Aimee. "Yes, but I miss

Alfie, too," she told me. While Aimee had taught her signing, it was Alfie who, before others, had delighted in her
mysterious signals. And she'd been intrigued by his indifference to the world's opinion of him at a time when she'd
almost ceded her own independence to "oralist prison."

We were better equipped to sort fact from fiction than
most reporters on the story. Alfie had been a powerless
queen in the CIA's rules-shifting chess game with the FBI,
training in female impersonation for a part in the grand
American comedy, that fear of sexuality and its attendant
hypocrisies. He'd been charged to spy on the FBI chief,
a night-sporting cross-dresser himself, whose files tagged
our ambassador to Russia as a security risk for the way his
tongue slid over his lips "in a feminine manner."

To think our Freak Corner had touched that wider
world of national intrigue in those months when fear ran
through our own house. I can see my father, watching Gayle
practice signing in front of her mirror. For him it was as
if she were advertising her availability. He'd recently been
pushed aside on the men's floor of his department store. He
traced the demotion to his failure to specify "no pleat up to
the belt line" in a large order for dress pants. The pants, "too
effeminate," had languished on the racks, unsold at half off.

GAYLE HAS GONE ON TO FAME in the tradition of Professor Stokoe, who taught her Chaucer while proclaiming the
completeness of American Sign Language and creating a
notation for its first dictionary. My sister dedicated her life
to the welfare of the profoundly deaf, spreading the news
of her own transformation. She became a world traveler for

signing, even lecturing at the campus that had once denied her an informal platform, Gallaudet University.

In spite of her efforts, it took Gallaudet, premier center of deaf education, another decade before accepting the truth of Stokoe's assertion that American Sign Language had its own grammar. And a decade more before a campus uprising established the principle of deaf leadership.

Her Ph.D. thesis asserted the administrators of a monumental institution like Gallaudet were not masters, but caretakers, and in 1988, on an arthritic hip, she marched with a thousand others from the campus to the university's board meeting across town, then to the White House, the Capitol, and back to campus, signing all the way "Deaf President Now."

Gayle's best-known work, *The Handicap of the Hearing*, through multiple editions and translations, circled the globe with a jolt for the world's majority, "sadly poorer, for the limitations of their spoken languages." It holds no recrimination for her parents, and no criticism for those whose fulfillment is immersion in the hearing world, but a warning: "Let no life be undiscovered, lost, or stolen by an aversion to signing, or to the joy in emotive, kinetic kinship it offers."

It seems a short way back to the afternoon Gregory Knox found my sister and me on our sidewalk. It was the day after we learned of Alfie's disappearance. Gayle signing her sorrow, and my own hands moving around my head, signaling confusion, had set Gregory off. He walked up, staring at our hand dance, calling me a "tool" and my sister a "cretin." He began to move his own hands around his head, twisting his mouth this way and that, mocking our silent conversation. Gayle's hands began to move faster.

"You having some kind of fit?" he asked her. She was repeating everything he said, turning mockery back on him in a dazzle of arms and hands, his bluster no match for its kinetic translation. She even signed his head-to-toe appraisal of her: "You wouldn't be so bad if your voice didn't squeak."

I circled a forefinger over the pursed ring made by the top of my fist (anus), then pulled a thumb from the bottom of the same clenched hand, signing's way of calling him excrement. Gayle pushed my hands aside. He wasn't worth our anger.

A few weeks later we watched the brothers drive off to ill-fated army enlistments with raised middle fingers, their departing message to the neighborhood. Gayle shook her head, not in disgust so much as pity for their impoverished vocabulary.

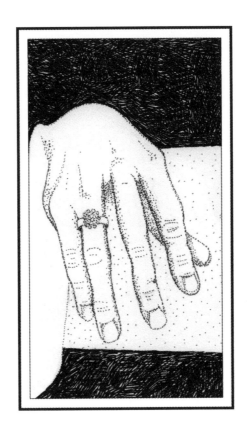

The diamond-decorated hand could as easily
have been in her lap.

THEIR GRANDFATHER'S CLOCK

THE CHILDREN'S MATERNAL GRANDFATHER, Major Clarke, was eighty-three when he came to visit his daughter Mary's family for the last time. This was in the hot, humid Virginia August of 1982, and the wild berry brambles and vines on the fencerows around the Wheelers' two acres made a wall up to eye level. Above that, branches of ailanthus and sumac laden with honeysuckle and poison ivy blocked a view of the Blue Ridge. Beyond these, on all sides, earlier property owners had let locust, cedar, and any other invasives run wild on the land.

The old farmhouse sat a hundred yards off the state highway. Its driveway led under the lowering branches of mulberry trees on either side, and once past these, enclosed in green, it seemed there might be no escape from nature's prison.

This was not suburban Virginia, but beyond that, where a drive-in theater survived in a land of scattered house lots where discarded tires painted white were used as planters. A few miles farther west, a roadside store advertised adult films and massage. Not much farther was a roadhouse where coal miners from West Virginia were known for weekend brawling.

Major Clarke with his second wife, Kokey, Mary's

stepmother, kept a tidy yard and bungalow in Rock Island, Illinois, where for years he'd volunteered as a docent at the Arsenal Museum. The Major had not forgiven Vincent for moving Mary and the children into their forsaken region of scarce and suspect neighbors, to a house Kokey thought little more than a dust and cobweb factory.

Vincent had been eager to leave the part of Virginia where home owners' associations and county governments harried and taxed a hapless population for a place where they could all relax into loose country clothing. They'd love it. The rustic refuge was half the cost of the tract house they'd left behind, and only a dozen miles from his work as a hydrologist in the Winchester laboratory where he analyzed the waters of the Shenandoah and Potomac Rivers.

Mary, forsaking her volunteer work at the public health clinic in Fairfax, was certain she'd find a similar use for herself in her new community. It hadn't happened. Too late she wondered, What could we have been thinking? Moving their three children from their trick-or-treat neighborhood to this rural wasteland, where their only social prospect was a deprived public school system. Any therapist could have predicted rebellion, bad humor, and family squabbles.

WITH THE VISIT ONLY A WEEK OFF, Mary saw that nothing was in order. Not the house, the yard, nor the children were ready for the arrival of her elderly father and his alert younger wife, whose inspections, more thorough than the Major's, could foretell cracks in a marriage from dust on a windowsill. She still wore the immodest diamond engagement ring of her first marriage. At sixty, young enough to be Mary's older sister; her coming, like a condescension of royalty. Why had her father married a woman who must prove every day that he couldn't afford her?

Any family pride in the Major's two-war military service had lost ground to his failing memory and loosened chronological bearings. Mary heard annoying irony in Vincent's references to "the Major." Her children giggled as they whispered "Bomp" and "Plokie," the family names for her father and his second wife, but she laid the coming trouble at the feet of her husband, and their ragged yard.

"The disrespect starts with you," she said. "When are you going to mow? The yard's a disgrace. You could make an effort."

She was right about the yard. It had been too wet to mow, then another week had gone by, and now the grass was over a foot tall, with locust shoots showing here and there. The children were out of patience with his orders, and the lawn mower, in a rebellion of its own, mute to every pull on the starter cord.

Susan, twelve, upset to be forced out of her bedroom by the visit, malingered in her window-cleaning assignment. Though confused and touchy in adolescent transition, she could hold her own against her brothers, Paul and Bennie, only eleven and nine but fully aware of her discomfort. She called down from an open window, "How many monkeys does it take to start that thing?" Paul knew better than to reply with a single finger while his father was watching.

"Hey! Sweater girl," he yelled back at her.

"Be quiet! All of you!" Mary called from the kitchen. "Don't be disgusting. You don't deserve to have a family."

Vincent, reassessing, knew that even if the mower

started, it would choke out before cutting a first swath. He phoned their man with a tractor to come with his bush hog and get the grass down to manageable length. And he called a family meeting. He'd seen this before—Mary's panic before a visit by the Major, and the family thrown into a bickering tailspin.

Before their kitchen council was over, the boys had pledged to stop exploring their sister's bureau, and to speak no more of her training bra; Susan would stop calling her brothers "Chimp" and "Chump," and Mary had a promise from Vincent that he'd go alone to pick up the Major and Kokey at the bus station in Winchester. To show his particular interest in their visit.

Mary, though conceding nothing, vowed to herself she'd show her stepmother a sincere welcome. But beyond her best intentions were the inescapable realities. The inevitable spark and ultimatum, damage and repair, then peace at senior nap time. Maybe a whole day between blowups, interludes of stifled resentment. She thought of Kokey's diamond-decorated hand on the dinner table beside the Major's place mat, a hand that could as easily be in her lap.

THE FAMILY RETURNED TO THEIR CHORES, but a few minutes later Susan was sitting at the top of the stairs, staring at nothing. Seeing her sullen expression, Mary mourned her daughter's lost moments of glad grace, once so easily shared. What if this were more than a phase? The year before, one of her classmates at the middle school had destroyed herself. Oh, the sweet innocence of a daughter whose Family Life class had jumped so far ahead of a mother's counsel: "Mom, what do you say when you want Dad to put seeds in you?"

"That's private, dear," leaving so much to a troubled imagination.

Distrusting her parents' claim for her natural beauty, Susan eclipsed the issue with blue hair and a heavy hand with eye shadow, which Vincent thought made her look like a raccoon in need of sleep. Now she was standing beside her bicycle in the driveway, a balloon-tired clunker with a single gear. She'd been waiting all summer to call herself thirteen. To put more distance between herself and her brothers, now a few actual miles. She looked balefully around at them in that shaky moment when wheels are hardly turning.

"Let her go," Vincent advised.

Mary put aside her morbid musing and turned to the realities, in particular her father's wandering mind. Hanging on to a conversation, the Major might mumble words, repeating them until his next thought arrived. It made the children uncomfortable to sit in the same room with him, only to be scolded if they dared to laugh.

When he "took a spell," he could fall into historical confusion, cutting an event from one decade and replacing it in another, his time traveling so smooth, you might fear for his safe return to the moment. If corrected too abruptly, he went to the piano in the parlor and played the "Battle Hymn of the Republic" at surprising volume and without a misplaced note. How about that, people? Mary could say to herself.

Susan, defeated by the first small hill, was back in fifteen minutes, and working again on the windows while the boys weeded the garden and their father straightened up a messy toolshed. Later, Vincent said the day's efforts were worthy of a night out for dinner. Paul and Bennie lobbied for Tyrana-Tacos at Dinosaur Land. Mary and Susan feared Vincent was thinking of the Caverns Diner, where a dwarf who did the chores had climbed into the booth beside them to recite the specials. Bennie had started crying, embarrassing everyone.

And God forbid, not popcorn at the ancient drive-in theater where Mary had once sat for two hours, embarrassed for her family as Doris Day smiled chastely over a congregation whose windows fogged all around them. Mary begged to go somewhere they wouldn't feel like cultural anthropologists. Vincent turned the car east, toward nationally advertised hamburgers.

VINCENT MET THE OLD FOLKS at the baggage retrieval inside the depot. There were arm's-length hugs and Kokey's "Hello, stranger! Where are the children? I suppose they had important things to do."

After several revolutions, they were staring at the only bags left on the carousel.

"Those can't be ours."

"Don't be silly. . . . His sight's going."

On the drive back as the roads narrowed, the Major leaned forward in the backseat to remind Vincent, "You moved her a long way out." Kokey allowed he was taking them the scenic way: "It can't be much farther."

After a silence too long to ignore, the Major offered, "Well, he stood up to Khrushchev, didn't he?" Vincent couldn't say. "Anyway, he's got inflation under control. Are you still testing river water? Well, look at that!", distracted for a moment by a cow grazing with her calf in a front yard.

"They're painted on boards," Kokey explained to him. "It's their art."

This could be all right, Vincent thought. If he just held back as a friendly chauffeuring presence, roadside attractions would entertain them. His heart softened and he apologized silently for his part in their alienation. He might have softened further had he known that a year later the Major's heart, on a schedule of its own, defying heroic measures, would stop forever.

As country landmarks slid by—the green machinery of the Deere outlet, a duck's wings decorating the side of a mailbox spinning in the wind, a volunteer fireman sitting beside the Stonefield station house—the surrounding vegetation thickened, branches lowered over the road ahead, and when they finally passed under the mulberry canopy and were in the Wheelers' yard, Kokey asked, "But where are the mountains?" And the Major was hardly exaggerating when he replied, "Where's the sky?"

The bush hogging had gotten the grass down to a half foot, but looking down, Kokey drew an audible breath, grabbed the Major's arm, and, lifting her dress with her other hand, went high-stepping across the lawn as if negotiating a hay field. The Major, hurrying ahead with her, seemed eager to leave Vincent behind and get on to blood relations. Mary, standing in the doorway, turned to hush one of the boys, who was arguing with his sister.

First thing, Kokey had to give Paul and Bennie their presents, yo-yos, which, without sleeper strings, met unenthusiastic gratitude. Susan would have to wait till the birthday party for her gift.

"Thank you?" Mary suggested.

"For what?" Susan asked.

The Major's solemn appraisal of his granddaughter— "quite the little lady"—maybe a wistful recognition she would never again sit in his lap to be tickled, perhaps matured beyond his ability to amuse her at all.

Mary led them up to Susan's room, where they'd stayed before. It had the queen-size bed and firm mattress the Major required. As in all the upstairs rooms of the old farmhouse, there was a cast-iron grate in the floor with a sliding baffle, allowing heat to rise through the house. Open, it made a sounding board, amplifying conversation in the kitchen below. "These can be so annoying," Mary apologized, bending down to be sure the vent was shut.

"Don't close that, dear," Kokey said. "That's how we know when the coffee's on," as if unaware of the antique fixture's bonus as family spyware.

ON DAY TWO OF THE VISIT, before others were up, Vincent drove into Winchester to negotiate with the dealer who'd sold him his mower two summers before. His rehearsed story of tall grass and in-laws held no weight against an expired warranty. But Vincent, sure that awakened combustion was only a few confident steps away, returned with a new condenser, a set of points, and a manual with a diagram of the mower's engine.

Walking into his house, he found the Major and Kokey huddled together on the sofa, holding hands in front of the television, seeking comfort from the available signal from Charlestown, half drama, half snowstorm. Drawing him into the kitchen, Mary explained how the day had started with Susan coming down to the breakfast table in the T-shirt that said "Boogie Till You Puke," with its photographic demonstration.

"Go to your room and take that off," the Major ordered. Instead, Susan rode away again on her bicycle, and the old folks retreated to their room.

From there the Major had gone exploring in the attic, where he found an honest-to-goodness squirrel's nest under the eaves. Bennie, who couldn't hide his amusement at a third repetition of "honest-to-goodness," was given a time-out. Enjoying his release from the difficult attendance on his grandparents, he never asked for an end to his confinement, and the punishment drifted away, beyond anyone's concern.

Vincent's commiseration with Mary was brief; he needed the remaining daylight to fix the mower. Easy enough, he thought. With the engine's cover removed, he saw again how clever the engineering of the thing for one with the cunning to appreciate it. Pleased with his swift accomplishment, he was pulling the starter cord with all the pride of a man who knows his way around a small engine. He choked and pulled and pulled, unchoked, and pulled and choked again and pulled, twenty-five times, maybe thirty, without a cough from "this fucking thing," and his frustration, "Shit, shit" and "Shit!" reached ears in the house.

At dinner, the Major, who had dreamed the two-week visit into completion in his afternoon nap, said it had all been very nice, he was grateful they had shown Kokey such a genuine welcome, but too bad they'd missed Susan's birthday party.

"No, no, Daddy," Mary said, correcting him gently. "You've only been here two days. Susan's birthday is next week."

"Well, it was all very nice anyway," he said, turning for confirmation from Kokey, who said, "You're tired, dear. We'll have an early night." She swiveled slowly under the family's gaze and, with no intention of mending the Major's confusion in front of this audience, rose to lead him up to bed. After tucking him in, she came back downstairs to confront the family.

"Go to your rooms," Vincent ordered the children.

"No," Kokey said. "Why shouldn't they hear this? I can imagine what you tell them about me." She sat opposite Mary to say her piece. "I see the way you stare at my hand, the way you all stare at it. If you'd like to know, the Major asked me to wear the ring. He demanded I wear it. Ask him. He said he couldn't respect a woman who didn't still love a husband she'd lost. Maybe his heart's bigger than yours." She turned to Susan, holding out her hand. "You can touch it, dear," she said. "It won't bite." Susan looked to her mother for permission.

"If you want to," Mary said, but Kokey had already withdrawn her hand.

Astonished, they waited for Mary to defend herself, to defend them all. She wouldn't be stared down by Kokey, but her silence seemed a defeat, a disappointment. Kokey went up to join the Major. No one spoke until Vincent said, "Well, that let the air out."

"Yeah, out of her butt," Paul said.

They were all looking to Mary for a reproval. All she said was, "He'll grow up."

Susan, in disbelief at the uncensured rudeness, said, "We should all grow up. You, too, Mom."

"WHAT'S TO DO AROUND HERE?" Kokey asked the next morning, as if she'd just arrived, as if they were starting all over again. "Any attractions?"

"A Family Dollar, eight miles," Mary said, surely a guarantee against excursion.

"We could have a look at that," the Major said.

"Not today," Vincent interrupted. After taking two days off in honor of the visitors, he was returning to work. No family trips until the weekend. That night, he returned from Winchester, excited to explain the impact his laboratory was having on the region's waterways, saving the details for the dinner so the Major and Kokey might better appreciate the significance of his work.

With all seated at table, he began: "Does anyone know what a PCB is?" The desired silence was broken by the Major's promise of "a little secret" if the boys would take their elbows off the table. Alert to their surreptitious pestering of their sister, he was missing most of Vincent's account of the perfidy of the country's largest rayon manufacturer in nearby Front Royal, the spilling of toxins into the Shenandoah River, the government's enforcement dereliction, a company spy discovered in his own laboratory, his counter-ploy, altering the water-testing schedule, and at last, this week, a consent decree signed by the polluters.

Kokey was confused. Mary tried to help: "It means

the company agreed to stop what they hadn't been doing."
The Major, meeting Vincent's waiting gaze, said, "Very
impressive, I'm sure."

THAT SATURDAY AFTERNOON, the whole family climbed
into the station wagon for the outing to the Family Dollar,
where Vincent and the boys, already wishing they were
home again, never got out of the car. Susan had a plan
to separate her mother from Kokey, whom she hoped to
wheedle into buying her a mood ring. Kokey led the way
into the store, where she pulled a large-sized shopping
cart from its rank and pushed off, alarming Mary, who
hurried to keep up with her.

"That older boy of yours is fresh as paint," Kokey told
her as Mary caught up.

"His name is Paul. Where are you going? What did
Paul say to you?" For the moment, both of them forgetting
the Major, who was ambling off on his own for a conversation with the pharmacist about blood thinners.

"Never mind what he said. You need to brighten up
that kitchen of yours." Kokey was pushing down a second
aisle, then a third. Coming to housewares, she began to
fill her cart. First with some dish towels with a house-
blessing message, then a powerful floor soap "for that
stained linoleum."

"To perk up the drawers and cabinets," she was counting out rolls of contact paper before Mary began putting all
of it back on the shelves. There was a brief tug-of-war for
the last roll. Kokey turned to some startled shoppers behind

her, as if they might pull with her. "You can lead a horse to water," she stage-whispered to them.

"Where's your father?" she asked, suddenly turning away. Both abandoning the cart, they went off in opposite directions, each hoping to be first to tell the Major what had happened.

The visit proceeded with the predicted bruises from sharp elbows. With only a few days left and scant prospect of new connection between her children and her father, Mary turned her attention to Susan's party. There was a secret after-work shopping trip to Winchester, but again it was "The lawn, Vincent," a trimmed lawn required for the grill and picnic table party.

THE MAJOR AND CHILDREN were standing over Vincent, who was on the ground beside the mower. The Major turned to Bennie: "Does your father know if it's not ignition, the problem is carburetion?" Vincent, who was already loosening the carburetor's bolts, told him to "move out of my light, please."

With the disassembled part in hand, he saw the problem at once: "A hole in the diaphragm."

"You mean we'll have another little mower?" Susan asked.

Paul shoved his sister hard in the chest for her stupidity. Vincent looked up in suspicious wonder at the sudden precocity of his daughter, who was yelling, "Did you see what he did to me?" Too much for the Major, who exploded, "What the hell is wrong with you people?" Pulling Paul and Bennie aside, he ordered them to go with him.

"Do as he says," Vincent told them.

Reluctantly, they followed their grandfather into the house and up to his room. The women, seeing it all from chairs on the porch, watched them enter the house. Hearing them troop up the stairs, Mary went into the kitchen, where she might listen to any conversation above without intruding. Susan, seeking commiseration, came over to join Plokie on the porch.

Above her, Mary heard her father yelling, "Sit there, both of you."

There was a squeaking of springs as they plopped onto the bed.

"Paul, you're the older one; where's the example? You should be ashamed, teasing your sister about her breasts." The boys saw the Major's eyes begin to wander left and right, as if he were suddenly lost. He looked down at them, found his place, and began again. "I've heard your farting noises. Listen, there are stinks in this world you never dreamed of. A soldier with his leaking guts in his hands There's a smell for you."

Paul saw an opening. "Weren't you an ambulance driver? Weren't you too young to be a soldier?"

Her father would recognize the adult tutoring behind this impudence. Mary could imagine his face turning red, hovering over her boys, forced into the past. "Your father doesn't know a thing about war. How could he in this day and time, when they decide which war they'll fight?"

His voice calmed and his mind went drifting behind trenches in France. "I didn't know the other drivers would be your poets and such.

"Do you know what you could catch in the Marne River?" He stopped for a moment.

From the kitchen, Mary could hear Susan on the porch, thanking Plokie again for getting her the mood ring. She was asking, "Is your ring very expensive?"

"No, dear. It's not the kind they find. It's the kind they make."

If she moved to hear more of this, Mary would be missing the news that was falling again from above, history her father had never shared with anyone. His anger gone as quickly as it arrived, he was telling the boys about the nurse Annemarie, who smelled like eucalyptus and had "one of those things with her mouth, a harelip. She thought she was my mother."

"Sit still. I'll tell you what you could catch in that river . . . a German hand . . . common as carp, all white and swollen, with stuff coming out of the thumb."

Mary was ready to run upstairs and put an end to this, but her father had calmed, and however horrid, his rambling was priceless history.

He went on: "Annemarie wouldn't let me out of her sight. She sat beside me, with the doctor in back. They called him a doctor. Didn't know lice from fleas. She knew all the roads . . . grabbed the wheel if she didn't like the way I was turning. . . ."

He hesitated, maybe losing his place or wondering why he was talking at all.

On the porch, Kokey was making Susan promise she wouldn't wear the shirt anymore, "the one that upsets your grandfather. . . . Do you like living so far from any neighbors?"

"It's not so bad," Susan lied. She didn't want to say how she and her brothers were bullied by a rougher sort of children on the school bus. "I think I have this friend, but he doesn't know my name. . . . I heard you yelling at Bomp last night."

"Did I wake you? Men can be very selfish."

"Plokie, are you and Bomp going to be burned? Or buried like you are?"

"We'll be cremated, dear. After they take what they want. We're both organ donors. They won't use his eyes because of the glaucoma."

"Well, I don't want to be burned."

"Don't worry about that. You've got a birthday coming."

Susan came in to get Plokie a glass of water. Mary went to the fridge. "No," Susan snapped at her. "You know she doesn't like ice in her water."

Mary sat back in disbelief. Her father still pestered the woman's sleep? Now he was wandering again behind French lines, where the hospital's carrier pigeon, Major Feathers, was still alive after twenty-three missions.

"They made her a gold medal, but she went missing before they put it on her cage. . . .

"A tree jumped out of a hole in the ground and scared me out of my proper head. I messed my trousers. They said it was a miracle I was still alive and they gave me a medal, too. . . .

"I was driving another doctor then. . . . The first was dead. . . . The new one told Annemarie to take her hand off my knee while I was driving. She paid no attention."

Moments later the Major was back in that hot Virginia August, teaching the boys how to play "I'm the King of the Castle, and You're the Dirty Rascal," climbing onto the bed with them, all laughing as he pushed them onto the floor. By the time Mary got upstairs to put an end to the roughhousing, the game was over. Her father was giving each of them a dollar bill, telling them to get something nice for their sister.

Shocked by the unfiltered horror but pleased with the way he'd put their puny scatology to rout, she stood motionless, and heard Kokey climbing the stairs to join him for their nap, maybe to share their new and privileged knowledge of the children.

Already groggy, lying on the bed, the Major was drifting three decades forward from his duty in France to a bunker on the New Jersey shore, spotting German planes. Before falling all the way into afternoon slumber, he confessed as the women removed his shoes and put a pillow under his head, "We never saw a German plane. We saw our own tankers exploding on the ocean."

Mary supposed the raucous voices she heard outside must be Vincent cursing his mower a half dozen ways. But at a window, she saw him lying in his hammock. Beyond the abandoned machine, crows settling on the lawn were squawking at some opportunity or danger.

Vincent roused himself and drove off to Winchester again for the mower's replacement part. Mary sat alone in the kitchen, grateful for the bland honor of her steadfast husband, whose birth year kept him exempt from all wars. But diminished, too, with nothing comparable of passion, vileness, disgrace, or triumph to be locked away against future examination, his life on trial, and his children in the jury.

When the old folks woke, the boys were upstairs again, pestering their grandfather to show them his medal. If it existed, Mary had never seen it.

THE NEXT MORNING, with Vincent hurrying to keep up, the mower rolled forward, roaring its release from human abuse, spraying grass to the side and, swath by narrow swath, preparing the lawn for Susan's celebration. Vincent nodded toward the porch, answering the cheers for his heroic achievement. When the satisfactory machine was stowed in the shed again, Kokey came out to ask, "Is someone going to rake the grass?"

AFTER THE PRACTICAL GIFTS were opened—a dress, a pair of jeans, a sweater—Susan looked wistfully to her father, supposing she could expect no more birthday gratification than any other adult, his cue to roll out her real present, a three-speed Schwinn, sky-blue, with headlamp, horn, and magneto. Attached to the handlebars, his card said, "To take you where your ring turns purple," though he feared it might do just that. Her eyes teared and the boys knew she was still one of them.

Susan was still riding it up and down the driveway, learning how to shift gears, when the sun went down. Paul, with Bennie in tow, had been following their newly imagined grandfather through the house—the one who messed his pants when a tree jumped out of the ground. "Show us your medal," they begged.

"Who told you about any medal?"

They took the first opportunity to go rummaging through his bureau.

Mary's love for her father could gather no credible case against Vincent's explanation of "the subconscious creativity" of a "self-promoting fabulist, too young for the first war and too old for the second," and "confused about which one he was fighting." With the facts against her, she slept in a separate room that night, before they drove the Major and Kokey back to the bus station.

Two thank-you notes, both written by Kokey, were a month in coming, one addressed to Paul and Bennie, one to Susan. The boys' note apologized for the week-long inconvenience of a shared bathroom, and held two five-dollar bills, the remarkable treasure outweighing any sting of censure for their "rude noises."

Susan's, more letter than note, held no financial reward, but raised her to a privileged sisterhood. "I hope you'll come to visit. Your grandfather isn't the fright he pretends. He actually likes your brothers. He says they're full of piss and vinegar. It's a compliment."

Plokey's list of things to do in Rock Island was not promising: "The Arsenal Museum, you wouldn't care for it. I shouldn't tell you, but the best thing we have here is the bridge to Davenport.

"You'll have your own room. You can see the Mississippi from your window.

"You might like the arboretum." Then, "Don't worry too much about your father's mistakes. Men are happy if they can keep a lawn mower going."

Finally, "You have your mother's eyes and nice skin.

Don't blame her for being rude to me. Remember she had her own mother."

For Susan, she signed herself "Kokey."

Susan did not flaunt her special standing in Rock Island, nor keep it a secret. She placed the letter, open, on the kitchen table, intending her parents should read it. They felt no shame in obliging her. Afterward it was filed in the hall secretary, like a cable between countries on either side of them, first among records of a new family diplomacy. It was soon joined by home-inspection reports, school transcripts, and contingent sale documents, all these after a kitchen council that began with the confession of their foolish foray into foreign territory and ended with a pledge of a retreat to the homeland.

He looked at the proffered hand, and asked his wife
how long the boy would be staying.

VIRGIN SUMMER

AT EIGHTEEN, JUST OUT OF HIGH SCHOOL, and lately besotted with my classmate Heather, I was no longer keen about a summer in France. A few months earlier I'd been Pierre, an eager applicant to the new Youth Abroad program, and accepted as a worthy candidate for cultural exchange. Vouched for by French and history teachers, passport at hand, and awaited by a host family in the Auvergne, I balked and was Peter again.

My parents, once suspicious of a youthful wanderlust, threw my earlier arguments back in my face. The paraphrasing of Kipling: What knows he of America who only America knows? And Twain: Cast off the bowlines, sail away from safe harbor. I'd pled my case too well. Beyond adolescence, I was ready for the Continent. Only a dozen years after World War II, it was still our duty to reach abroad, to show the young American face, even one with the occasional pimple, to teach and be taught by a transatlantic culture.

Wherever I'd heard all this, in the end, there was no reneging. My preparation, which included a third year of high school French, now forced me to the pier in New York and drove me toward the gangplank of a seedy-looking passenger liner.

At dockside, I suffered through introductions *en français* to my travel companions. We gathered around a man identified by a red bow tie, who passed us on to one of our ship's junior pursers, our guardian for the crossing. He was to see that the even dozen of us were met in Le Havre by our French tour leader. The others, seven girls and four boys, all older college students, were chatting in an easy French far beyond my conversational skill.

Alarmed at the prospect of a strict French-only summer, I could follow but not really join the two discussions going forward. There was talk of our ship's history with misgiving as to seaworthiness. Two boys were going on about postwar politics in the Auvergne region.

For me it was achievement enough that I understood the ship had once been a troop carrier, had sustained the bankruptcies of several owners, had once been called the *American Banker*, and now sailed under a Greek flag. All agreed the dark brown staining on its white-topped hull, nearly obscuring the ship's identity—*Arosa Kulm*—was not reassuring.

As we hoisted duffels and climbed up over the dark water, a boy whose voice dominated the boarding party declared his excitement to be visiting a country thrown into a fascists' fire, burned to its republican roots, but now blooming again, a flourishing democracy. They had withstood a terrible onslaught, and emerged with their honor intact. We were lucky to be on our way to witness the triumph of de Gaulle.

This before we were even on the main deck. And when we were properly aboard, resting for a moment beside our luggage, he chose my lowered eyes for a target. *"Après tout,"* right in my face. *"Pensez de l'affaire Blum. . . . Une débâcle pour Vichy. A Riom, n'est-ce pas? Comprenez?"* Obviously for my benefit alone, in French so slow, even I could translate, he explained, yes, Riom, our summer's destination, had been home to the show trial of the three-time socialist prime minister Léon Blum for prewar treason, which became a public relations disaster for the Vichy government.

I disliked this lecturing prig Kevin, even before we'd exchanged names, before a good look at his unfortunate overbite or the roll of fat over his belt could influence my opinion of him.

I knew nothing of the political winds in Riom, past or present. To me, Riom was only the town where we'd meet our French families. Turning away, I said, "No," I didn't know. Not *non* but no, already breaking the French-only rule, wondering aloud, in English, where the purser was, and who would show us to our cabins. I was disappointing some of them, but a dark-haired girl, an inch or two taller than I, with a lovely open face, moved to my side, put a reassuring hand on my arm, and introduced herself as Charlie from Asbury Park.

"You didn't understand," she said. "There aren't any cabins for us. Just dormitories, boys' and girls'." She explained again, this had been a troop ship, not a luxury liner. The others tried to force me back into French, but Charlie was my immediate ally. If Kevin had been sent to spoil the voyage, maybe she was there to save it.

All the way across the Atlantic, while Kevin and others condescended—"When you have the subjunctive in hand, the rest will fall into place"—Charlie joined me in cheating. The very first night aboard, after a steam-table dinner in the common cafeteria, when our troupe retired to the recreation hall on the boat deck, debating landscapes *"après Poussin,"* and the bourgeois obstacles to French socialism, Charlie and I escaped to an upper level. Side by side at the rail, we let our contraband exchange be erased in the breeze.

She did say I'd have to try harder, that I had to get ready for my French family, who might be ordinary country folk without a word of English. But she didn't wince like the others if I stammered for a simple noun, or retreated into English. Very quickly she guessed the source of my further distance from the group.

"Peter," she said, out of the blue, "by the end of the summer you won't even remember her name."

To that end, she took my hand in hers and did a half turn, raising my arm around her shoulder so that we were joined side by side, looking down over the rail at the mysteries of the passing sea. I felt no sense of attack, no need to pull away, intrigued by her detachment from the group's mission, her awareness of something unbalanced in our group's superior leisure to observe the ordinary French *en famille.*

She wondered if I was from a wealthy family, as most of the others seemed to be.

No, but comfortable. My father, I explained, was admired among friends as one who'd turned away from wealth to serve the country. He'd been president of the American branch of a British shipping company, knowledgeable about things like the draft lines painted on the hull below us, maritime insurance, and the price of Brazil nuts shipped from the Amazon, but had gone to Washington from New York in 1941 to work for the government in procurement of war materials. From there he'd joined the State Department and eventually the Foreign Service. I'd had no answer for his pious farewell. "You'll be an ambassador this summer. Do us proud."

Charlie edged closer, and confessed to a late discovery of her family's wartime selfishness. She'd always known her parents despised Roosevelt, but had only recently learned how her father had made the most of the war in a shady foreign corner of the rubber market, out of sight of U.S. prosecutors. She said what she knew now could have sent him to jail. Her father's summertime good-bye had been "Remember who's paying for this nonsense. Not the government."

It wasn't clear why she'd offer me such damning information, but I was happy to be spirit mate of this older girl, whose openness put the guarded high school conversations, the immature dance around sex that I'd left behind with Heather, into sorry relief. On the remaining evenings of our crossing, we sneaked bottles of English beer out of the mess, carried them up to the same place at the rail, and took subversive pleasure in our alienation from the group. Opposing confessions, mine of wartime pieties, hers of greed, only strengthened our bond. On our last evening at the rail, we let our empty beer bottles fall on the canopy of a lifeboat hanging below, and watched them bounce off into the sea; we were renegade bombardiers on a mission of our own.

"Let your crew cut grow out," she advised me. "Grow some hair on your lip." As it was, I was fit to frighten the Continent with my compulsive American grooming. "And go a little easy on the deodorant, or shaving lotion, or whatever it is. Not useful," she said. "In France it just works against you." I should keep in mind Napoléon's note to Josephine: "Home in two weeks. Don't wash."

I wasn't insulted, but freshly in awe, brought up short mainly because there wouldn't be time for the complete makeover. There were five days and nights of shipboard revelation, Charlie leading me across the water, past the magical worlds of her diaphragm, and her period, into shameful secrets of her social diary. With all that, no urgency for consummation between us, and there was none. There might have been, she said, had there been cabins instead of dormitories. But hadn't our honesty with each other passed common intimacy, as if sex for us was already a take-it-or-leave-it sort of thing? She made it seem exciting that we'd jumped over it with our feet never touching the ground.

It was Kevin, at mealtimes, who led the weightier discussions. Topic A: morality as perceived on the Continent. From him I heard the word *existentialism* for the first time, and none too soon for the summer ahead, where it was in such currency in cafés and bars, it might have been mistaken for the name of the language spoken in France. Kevin assumed we'd all been trained against religious convention, that we believed mankind had found its moral code without need of a law-giving God. I wouldn't admit I hadn't thought much about it. Our moral authority was our own conscience as taught by the evolution of a thousand generations, Kevin said. If this was glib, it was also preparation for the summer ahead, inoculation against the mores of the family waiting for me in Riom.

Before we docked in Le Havre, a telegram was delivered from the ship's radio room. My parents: "Make the most of it, Peter. Heather says no word from you. Why don't you wire her from the ship?"

We were met by our French tour leader, Monsieur Pettigaud, minister of Riom's only Protestant church. He spread his arms like a conductor, against wandering, and his lips moved from one to twelve, counting us over and over again as he led us through customs and immigration. He was behaving like the headmaster of a primary school, but with the exaggerated movements of a man not quite sober.

At the railroad terminal in Le Havre, we crowded into several second-class compartments for Paris. Pettigaud closed the doors on us, and went forward to some accommodation of his own. Most of us slept on that first leg to Paris. At sometime on the ocean crossing, the de rigueur French summer must have exhausted vocabularies, or patience. Or maybe the others needed respite before the ultimate test of their competence in the all-French households of the host families.

Kevin was reading aloud in English from the *Paris Tribune*, a notice from Auvergne: Venom in the Palais de Justice in Riom. A feud that would not die. Reputations challenged. Two libel suits in progress. Typical of journalism everywhere, Kevin said, making a headline out of trivia. Meanwhile, Charlie was preparing me for our separation, explaining how close two people might come, only to touch and bounce apart. She told me not to worry, we'd share news of our summer adventures when we convened with Pettigaud in Riom on the weekends. But the closer we came to that city, the more she was behaving like an older sister. That week she had licensed my imagination, never my hands. Between Montargis and Nevers, she fell asleep against my shoulder.

We changed trains for the last time in Saint-Germain. Pettigaud, who'd been traveling in dining cars all the way from Le Havre, came through the train to rouse us before we reached Riom. Our air was fouled from Gauloises cigarettes. A preference for the simple blue packets discovered on the crossing was a mark of the group's growing sophistication, stronger tobacco for recently informed existentialists. Pettigaud disapproved. He stood in the corridor between our compartments, fanning the smoke away from his nose, directing our gaze to the passing geography, the volcanic mountains of the Massif Central.

At the station we waited to be sorted into two vans and carried to farms in the surrounding countryside. Two of us were being met by hosts who lived close by and could provide their own transportation. Jennifer, one of the quietest in our group, was led across the platform and introduced to a Madame Principe and her daughter, Clemence. They stood beside a shiny sedan, surveying our motley of blue jeans, loose sweaters, a few prim tunics, loafers, and saddle shoes.

The woman was perhaps forty-five, in a little beret-style hat of blue silk decorated with two paper roses; her daughter, half that age, with no pretension to style, though like her mother she had cropped black hair, wore a high-buttoned white blouse and skirt of rumpled linen. They seemed hastily dressed, as if for a nearly forgotten chore. More like inconvenienced bourgeois than the generous provincials advertised by Youth Abroad.

Immediately Madame Principe was arguing with

Pettigaud. The Principes, we'd been told, were last-minute volunteers, taking the place of a family indisposed by a child's illness.

"We will not have a girl," Madame Principe told Pettigaud, as if he should have known better, even if he was only the Protestant pastor.

"My son!" she said, by way of explanation. "My husband! My God!"

"It was settled," Pettigaud insisted. Assignments were final.

"Never," she said. "Not in my house."

A little crowd was gathering around, and someone took up for Madame Principe as she came toward us, apparently to see what else was available.

"Let her choose."

"That one," she said, pointing at me. "We'll have him."

There were ultimatums. Voices raised, calmed, and raised again.

"Pierre's French is weak," Pettigaud told someone in the gathering audience, as if this might make its way back to Madame Principe's ear and prejudice her against me.

"He'll cause no trouble," she said. "Clemence, help with his luggage."

It was obvious. I was the youngest, guileless and bewildered, if a little vain at being chosen so swiftly.

Pettigaud was still remonstrating, but losing force, and by then the rejected Jennifer had told him she wouldn't care to go where she wasn't wanted. The daughter, Clemence, without a word to me, was loading my duffel into the trunk of their car. Charlie pulled me aside.

"Don't go with them," she said. Pettigaud hadn't the

authority to make the change, she told me, predicting I wouldn't be happy with these people. But how could she know that?

Once more the center of the group's concern, aware of the blood in my cheeks, I was eager to be away, perhaps a little guilty, imagining the comforts in the household of these determined women. Clemence held open the car's front door for me to sit beside her mother, who drove. I waved to the group waiting for their vans, and we were off to the Principes' country home, heading south on the road to Clermont-Ferrand.

Putting me in front, Clemence could watch my reaction to her questions.

"Americans," she said, "study foreign languages. Europeans learn them, isn't that so?" It took her less than the several-kilometer trip to their villa to prove it.

With her mother, it was the opposite. Impatient, her English weaker than my French, on home ground she expected the struggle to be mine. Madame Principe said living in the country was a great inconvenience. There was little to do, but I would find my own diversions. And to her daughter, as if I wasn't there, or couldn't understand: "*Là!* The hair. So short! Like a picture from the German camps."

"You chose him," Clemence reminded her.

The soft crunch of white gravel in their driveway, a fountain splashing over a bronze Winged Victory, the *porte cochere* on the restored stone farmhouse—all of these and my tacit complicity in the sudden right turn my provincial summer had taken were left unmentioned in a first letter to my family. I did describe the stenciled frieze of rabbit, hound, and hunter under the ceiling molding of my second-floor guest room. But not the king-size down-filled cloud I slept on in the wing shared by Clemence and her brother, Valton.

I couldn't think why Madame Principe had offered this plush room to Youth Abroad. There was no pretense here of particular interest or welcome. Monsieur Principe, a boss and chief procurement officer at the big tire company in Clermont-Ferrand, had moved them to the villa abruptly from a spacious house in Riom, according to Clemence, to escape the irritations of small-town life, the insults actually, she said, of jealous tradesmen and the like. Introduced to me, her father looked at my proffered hand, nodded, and asked his wife how long she meant for me to stay.

"As long as he wishes," she said.

The house was filled with ancient furniture, armoires and chests carved with astonishing dates, crests, and family trees. An extra leaf in the oak dining table turned their family circle into an oval for our first meal together, a salmon salad served by their maid, who went about her work silently, looking no one in the eye. With Madame and Monsieur at the ends, I on one side, Clemence and Valton on the other, we made an easily read picture of the new imbalance in the house.

Madame did not slow her French for me. "Of course," she said, "you have left someone special behind in America."

I replied with something like "It has passed not yet two weeks, and I can hardly remember to myself the name of her." And then, "I'd be very content to be acquainted with the butter."

That first night, after I retired, they argued in the hall outside my room. Monsieur had come over to the children's wing to open doors, to see the new situation for himself, and Madame followed to argue with him. "You're never here! Why should you care?" I heard Clemence tell them to go back to their side of the house. A door was slammed.

I wondered if I'd been added there to shake something loose, to turn a testy household into open conflict. It was Clemence who had seen Pettigaud's notice in a Riom patisserie, seeking a last-minute host. I imagined my arrival as an opportunity for their mischief, an irritant to be lodged under the father's roof. Each morning, after a sip of coffee, he was off in his Peugeot to the tire company. Madame Principe took a breakfast tray back to bed, before dressing and driving off in her own sedan to the longueurs of an unemployed day, who knew where.

The son, Valton, pretended indifference to me in front of his father. At fifteen, too young to drive and too old for his bicycle, he was picked up each morning by a friend from Riom, and followed his father's commute to Clermont-Ferrand, where he was doing research in the region's history library, adding summer luster to his school record. By his sister's account, most days he sneaked off to a young people's café to wait tables, making just enough to smoke and keep a jukebox going.

Clemence, too, went her own way. A little impish, a little dour, when speaking to me she did not hold my gaze. She had her own little car, and sprayed driveway gravel going and coming. No job, but a checkbook. The one who had favored my visit, she was not ignoring me exactly, maybe holding me in reserve till I might be more useful. I gathered from her phone conversations she had several young men vying for time beside her in her runabout. None of the Principes liked staying home.

On my second morning there, with Monsieur Principe gone, Valton led me to a garden shed behind the house. "For you," he said, pointing to the wide-tired bicycle he'd grown too sophisticated to ride. He described the bike's three gears, "slow, slower, slowest," on the hilly landscape to either side of their valley. He sketched a map that would take me in a circle to Riom and home again. Landmarks to note—the shanty of a woman who would walk into the road and stop me for palaver, the benches in Riom where I could sit and watch the municipal workers cleaning the latest graffiti from the walls around the Palais de Justice, and on the road back from town, a black dog, who would give chase for the last kilometer.

It was hard going on the back route to Riom, and the lady from the humble house was standing in the steep road as Valton predicted, with her hand raised against my passing, a crone in a scruffy shawl and black skirt to her ankles. She had only a few things to say but held my handlebar until she'd finished: "No hair! Lice? Fech! This is the Principe bicycle. Good! Keep it. I could tell you plenty about him." But she waved me off.

In Riom I rested awhile on one of Valton's recommended benches. Again he was right. Men were cleaning painted messages from the walls of the public buildings. Two young men in business suits sat beside me to eat bag lunches. They had questions about the Everly Brothers and the talking horse, Mr. Ed. When I asked about the scribble on the walls, I was put off, and when I persisted, the two of them walked off together. On the way home, the black dog I was warned about must have been sleeping.

In the house for the rest of the afternoon with only the silent maid for company, I went to my room with a pen and one-piece air letter, addressing Heather in a pinched hand, thinking my news for her would never fit. By mid-page I was writing an oversize script, stumped, wondering if I had the heart to fill the sheet. I might have guessed a description of Clemence would only be an irritation: "Attractive on the surface, outspoken to her family, though reticent with me. Very spoiled, twenty-three, finished with her education, no job, but her own money and her own little car, a Deux Chevaux, in which she comes and goes as she pleases. When criticized by her parents, she retreats to her room. So, you can see, not my type at all."

Though limited to Valton's bike for transportation, I did reach several hillside villages. The local folk found my presence amusing, my exertions on the hills especially so, since I was mute and virtually deaf in their dialect, and had no apparent purpose in achieving the steep ascents other than to stare back at them. It was a relief when Saturday came and I was driven to Riom by Madame to gather with the other Youth Abroad. She said I was to disregard Monsieur's bad humor.

In town, Charlie spilled over with hardship. Her night of arrival on her farm, she found she was to be in charge of two boys, five and three, her obligation in return for five weeks of the family's barnyard culture offered in a French she could scarcely understand. Then the sharp cries of a rabbit as Monsieur pulled it by the ears from its hutch, slit its throat, and butchered it for a welcoming stew. Her bed, she said, was a cot in a stifling garret. She had bites on her legs from something that might be living in the straw-filled tick.

Most of the rest seemed happy in their rustic situations, though Amy had puked after a vinaigrette of roast pork intestines, which her kitchen-proud hostess had made specially for her from a fifteenth-century recipe calling as well for liver, spleen, and tripe to be fried in sweet grease. She might have held it down, she said, if not made to hear the recipe after eating. It was a minor setback in the party's week full of farm tradition—introductions to lore and idiom that could not be found in dictionaries. There was an enthusiastic exchange of news, their evenings in the local *bar-tabacs*.

Apparently cosseted in my bourgeois family, I was to be pitied, outside the group's cohesive bond. The summer went on that way. Charlie came to terms with her mischievous charges, accepted her discomforts, and stopped threatening to leave. Meanwhile, I became more of a regional curiosity in my expanding cycling radius. Valton admired my new calf muscles.

On our third weekend, Pettigaud had nothing more to show us by walking the streets of Riom. We'd done the architecture, admired the basalt walls and red roof tiles; the Palais de Justice, the region's judicial center and venue of the infamous "war criminals" trial; the folk museum, and a museum of Roman artifacts. It was during that weekend gathering that Kevin pointed me to the faint remains of my host's name, Victor Principe, where it had been insufficiently scrubbed from a municipal building's wall. A shame, he thought, the way they would drag people's names into the streets, and deface their historic town.

One evening after a long silence around the Principe dinner table, Madame rolled her eyes back, then fixed them on her husband. "What do you expect us to do? Do you think we are deaf? Blind? Stay here? Are you insane?" Monsieur was livid. Son and daughter stared balefully at their father. The maid finished her serving and made an excuse for leaving the house early.

I woke that night to a chorus of family anger, and went barefoot to the top of the stairway, where I heard all four of them below me in the front hall. Husband and wife in a fury, the children pleading with them to stop. Madame attacking, Monsieur on defense: "You think there were heroes?" he said. "You're dreaming!"

"What else did you do?" Madame screamed "Is there more?"

"Heroes?" he said. "Socialists! Communists! Heroes?"

Madame was sobbing. I went to my room. Their phone rang several times, and there was more shouting, threats, the receiver slammed onto its hook. Sometime later I woke to Madame sitting on the end of my bed. She was stroking my feet through the bedclothes. I sat up; she pushed me back. "*Ecoutez*," she said. "You are scared?" Half French, half English, eager now for me to understand.

Yes, I was nervous, but she was truly afraid, her place on my bed evidence enough of her derangement, already at the heart of some justification, way ahead of herself.

"Madame Porte is a bitch! Her husband is a snake!"

I pulled my foot away from her massaging hand.

"What do you take me for?" she said. "What are you thinking? Anyway, you don't even know them!"

She gathered herself, and began again.

"Accommodation, collaboration, you understand the difference?"

"Yes."

"How could you? You weren't here."

I was helpless.

"My husband's name is on the Plaque of Resistance in Clermont-Ferrand! My sister's husband was sent east and died in the camp. Now this!"

She reached forward to pull at the sheet I hid behind.

The door swung open, and there was Clemence. She screamed at her mother, "What are you doing? Get off his bed! Get out of his room!"

Madame rose and strode past her daughter, waving her arms in innocent dismissal, as if this were someone else's problem. Minutes later I heard the front door slam. At my window, I could see Madame and Valton walking across the driveway, getting in her car, and driving away, south toward Clermont-Ferrand.

I had settled onto my bed again when Clemence returned to order me out of the house.

"You're coming with me," she said. "Put your things in the suitcase."

She didn't stay for my questions, but went to her room to pack her own bag, and when she came back, I was ready for whatever she had in store, thinking perhaps she was getting me out of there, away from her mother, for her own safe-keeping. She led me to the Deux Chevaux, we put our bags in the backseat, and off she drove, heading north. I gave no second thought to the other "youth abroad," or Heather, whose mailed response had been sharp and liberating.

I was obtuse, she'd written, telling me not to restrict myself on her account, that our mutual friend Stephen had been taking her to the pool and the occasional movie. Perhaps we'd talk when I got home. Perhaps not.

Done and done, and the road ahead of us went straight through the center of Riom.

"That was our house," she said, pointing to a massive corner residence. In her mother's family for generations. "No German ever walked through the door." She was proud that the Boche army had never billeted there. She circled the block, stopping on the second pass to look once more at the place where she'd grown up.

"Something did not walk well for you here?" My French was still hopeless.

"Don't be stupid," she said.

Out of town, she turned to the northeast, following signs to Vichy. It was after 2:00 A.M. when we arrived at the inn, where the keeper, she said, was a friend of her family. He was not annoyed, but embraced her when he opened the door, pulling her inside for her whispered explanations, interrupted here and there with his moaning empathy, and a final bear hug of assent when asked, "Is it possible? Can you make room for us?"

I was close on her heels as we went upstairs behind him, not prepared for the iron arm that fell in front of me as I tried to follow her through the opened door of a bedroom.

"Non! Qu'avez-vous?" Scandalized, he led me to another room from which I would use the bathroom at the end of the hall. I heard Clemence lock the door to her suite, and

did not see her till the next morning in the parlor, sitting at the coffee table, licking the crumbs of a croissant from her palm. I sat across from her.

"We'll go for a walk," she said. "First I call my brother to see what has happened."

"Then we'll drive home?"

"You are in a hurry?"

She made her call, and we set off down the street, a mile or so to the banks of the Allier, then downstream along the river, and she began to talk, just as her mother had: "Madame Porte is a bitch. Her son is a dunce, always behind Valton in school. Her husband is a snake. He takes orders from my father at the tire company, yet uses his parking space," as if the petty animosity was enough to explain the Principes' flight from their home in the middle of the night.

I caught her staring at me once, not admiring, evaluating; maybe not sure how much she could afford to tell me. "My father," she said, "blew up two locomotives that might have been used for exportation. His name is on the Plaque of Resistance."

She turned us back into the town, and told me it was too soon to go home; we would stay there at least one more night. Familiar with the place, she led us to Vichy's oldest spa, where she sat me on a park bench and went inside for a full thermal treatment with massage, leaving two hours for me to wander where I would. Afterward, there was a café where she ordered for both of us—wine, salad, and a chewy loaf to soak in our snails' garlic butter.

I made no protest when our visit stretched to a third night. Clemence was treating me like a pathetic little brother who could make her life unbearably tedious. Her confessions came with plentiful excuses. After all, her father had been a hero of the Resistance, hadn't he? Each night the innkeeper came up to see that her door was locked against me.

Before we drove home, the damage had been done. Every window on the ground floor of the Principe home had been smashed and thrown rocks had found the second-floor glass. The massive front door had been splintered by a battering log that must have taken half a dozen men to propel. There was a rope across the driveway, and a police-man staked out there, who told Clemence she would find her family, though perhaps not her father, at a pension in Clermont-Ferrand.

My escape with the Principe daughter put an end to the Youth Abroad summer. The organization, frightened by my reported absence, wary of legal problems, ordered all of us home. We were rounded up by Pettigaud a week early, and driven all the way to Le Havre, to make the Arosa Line's next sailing. I was ignored in the van; there were asides about my thoughtlessness, my self-indulgence, a girl's reputation—the men less censorious than the women, though with nothing to say to me.

I boarded the *Arosa Star* in the mantle of a careless player who'd had my way with France, though scarcely competent in the language, and was now sneaking home without remorse, without consequence. Kevin couldn't believe it. "She paid for everything? The room? The restau-rants? The spa?"

Two days into the return passage, Charlie softened. She brought her lunch tray to sit beside me in the cafeteria. Her silence was a cue to begin.

"The Principes only had me for protection," I told her. As if the presence of an American might keep Monsieur's enemies away from the house. "He had a lot of enemies, who were just then being reminded of their quarrel with him." Not only Porte, his subordinate at Michelin, the same Porte whom he'd reported for workplace violations, and who, in return, had given him a full-arm gesture in the company parking lot. After that, it was war, past and future.

I didn't embellish the story, only repeated what Clemence had confessed in Vichy, how her father had named Porte in a libel case after Principe's name appeared among a list of collaborators still at large, painted on Riom's walls. A mistake, Porte countersued, and other antagonists awakened an old story of Principe's friendship with the Milice, the Vichy regime's paramilitary, hand in glove with the S.S. during the occupation. It might have died in the whispering but for the odd discovery of old files in a Riom attic, said to be miscellaneous records the Vichy puppets failed to destroy.

Charlie wanted the rest to hear this, but when she called them over, only Kevin and a couple of others bothered to move. Most still wanted nothing to do with me.

I began again with Clemence's story, her lament for her country: "Every time a name goes up on the French honor roll, someone comes out of the past to erase it."

Kevin inhaled deeply on a Gitane, a brand he'd chosen to distinguish himself from the group's Gauloises habit, and threw a weary hand into the discussion, as if to say, France, after all. What can one expect?

But I had their attention. Principe had been stung by a facsimile reproduction in a regional newspaper, under the heading WHO IS V.P.?, a penned note in the prosecutor's record from the Vichy's aborted show trial in Riom. Barely legible: "V.P. of M. will arrange a company statement against Blum." The cowards, Clemence said, wouldn't dare print Victor Principe of Michelin. They let gossip do their *merde*.

Worse, she admitted, had appeared just in the last week, discovered in the same Vichy files, this time clear enough. "No German officers to be quartered with V.P. of M., who knows local population and will assist with family genealogy." This was after German troops had marched into the unoccupied zone, Clemence explained. They were demanding laborers for exportation to Germany, then purifying all of France. Two Jewish grandparents were enough stain to send you to the Drancy camp near Paris. And from there, east in a cattle car.

My story told on the boat made its way through the rest of our group, disrupting the satisfaction taken in their taste of the real French family; vexed to think their pleasure in the custom and idiom of rural France had been taken unaware of the fire of memory and retribution burning underneath them.

I walked the decks of the *Arosa Star* alone, untroubled by the serial opportunism of my imagination, which had slept that summer with Heather and Charlie, and, most memorably, Clemence. Was her father still in flight, in search of a new name, a new family, a new country? If all she told me was fact, he had seen to it that neither a German officer nor his own wife's brother-in-law, among others he betrayed, would ever cross his threshold.

Embarrassed beyond tolerance, she put a hand
over his mouth.

THE MAN FROM TRENTON

TWO WOMEN BEGAN TALKING in the quiet car as soon as they boarded in Washington. They were still talking as the train did its unnerving balancing act over the Susquehanna. They were talking as they got off in Philadelphia. Why hadn't someone told them to shut up?

Eric Nolting, who winced at any cell phone's trill, was traveling with his wife to New York to defend his manuscript, "The Narcissism of Small Differences." He was relieved to see the women depart, still annoyed that no conductor had silenced them.

At Trenton, a determined young man came pushing into the car and sank into a seat across the aisle. He pulled his laptop out of its case, put the phone thing on his ear, and began. "David! Walt here. All good? No, take it off the agenda. I don't want Amanda at the meeting."

Nolting's wife, Denise, who hadn't read Eric's new book, knew it stole much from their married life, but her immediate concern was Eric's sudden defense of the silence promised in a quiet car. He was thinking aloud, "If Walt is so important, why did he get on the train in Trenton?"

She turned to block her husband's voice and view. Walt was saying he wanted David to take responsibility for the

Northeast region, leaning forward into the importance of his conversation.

Talking past his wife's warning eyes, Eric said, "What's Walt doing in the quiet car?"

Walt, whether unself-conscious or fully aware of his performance, was talking louder against the interference of this voice across the aisle. "No. I don't care what her figures are. Is she listening to this? Have you got me on speakerphone?"

Eric, ignoring his wife's poke in the ribs, answered the eager businessman. "You've got yourself on speakerphone."

But Walt had only gotten started. "No, don't send it back. Fix it yourself. Don't have Amanda do it. You do it."

"Roger," Eric called across the aisle.

Denise, embarrassed beyond tolerance, put a hand over her husband's mouth, which barely muffled "I say we lighten up, Walt? Let Amanda be Amanda."

With that, she pushed herself away from him, stood, and escaped to the club car, which meant Eric might have no supporting witness to the ensuing events. Unless the conductor who happened down the aisle as the train stopped at an empty place called Metropark might later say something in his favor, or the hastily summoned Homeland Security soldier, a corporal in camouflage, holding his weapon, barrel and trigger, over astonished passengers. Or maybe some unknown rider would have taken his side, if he'd thought to ask one.

The guardsman, inflated with sudden importance, was demanding picture identifications. The conductor took names. The man from Trenton, tapping Eric's information into his computer, had time to call over his shoulder as he was led to another car, "Get a life!"

Denise didn't return until the train made its ear-socking plunge into dim-lit silence under the Hudson River. She wouldn't sit down, looking away toward the car's exit. Minutes later, several blocks from the station, she was speaking to Eric only to remind him how angry she was. It was time for them to separate—he on his way up Madison Avenue to his agent, Denise continuing east to their hotel for aspirin and a lie-down.

"Careful with this," he said.

Reluctantly, she took their shared wheeled suitcase, which held the laptop, e-stuffed with his book and its several revisions. He had apologized to Denise for embarrassing her. He, of all people, should know an overheard conversation might be a writer's gold. What if he'd never heard the woman who slammed a receiver against a phone-booth door in Penn Station, announcing, "That's it! The straw is broken! The camel has had it!"? What if the conductor Sviatoslav Richter's comment to his second flute had never carried beyond the orchestra pit at Covent Garden: "Your damned nonsense can I stand twice or once but sometimes always my God never!"? Pearls like these were at the heart of Eric's smashing success with *Beyond Logic, Beyond Grammar.*

He hadn't confessed to his wife what he admitted to his agent—the way he'd bounced for the last six months between his email and Web search, hoping reluctant fingers could be lured to his Word program, even if met there by a blank screen. There was nothing new inside the silver machine. He was surprised how easily his agent obliged him.

"Look," Nathan explained, "it's natural to worry after a triumph, and what writer hasn't recoiled between confident kinship with his keyboard and a blockage? But this, the dead stop of a one-through-twenty-six alphabet allergy?

Before Eric met Denise, a therapist hired by the private academy where he'd been teaching American history had asked him, "What part of your trouble would you say was avoidable?" a tacit accusation of Eric's eavesdropping habit. He met the insult by indirection, affecting shame for Aquarian parents whose treacly affection for each other he called "sugar diabetes." "They had noses for each other like magnetic Scotties."

Which begged the man's next question. Why had he been living with parents so far past a normal move-on date? Already seven years out of college, sliding through another year of Founding Fathers, hard currency, and Civil War, when suddenly his principal wanted a psychiatric evaluation.

Eric met the examiner's absurdity with more of the same, eagerly describing life in his parents' cramped house, where he was used to waiting outside the only bathroom while they shared a morning toilet. The gargling, the hawking, the groaning plumbing—flesh and pipe—the splashing in the sink and bowl, and his appeal, "How much longer?"

"You'll have to wait. Your father's on the stool."

"Can you imagine?" he asked the psychologist. "When I tried again, my mother said, 'He thinks there may be a second delivery.' Both in there and she's splashing over the sink, doing something to herself with a washrag."

The man had heard enough. Eric was not shown his report, but it sat on the principal's desk, where he could steal a glimpse.

Eric Nolting, age twenty-seven, American history instructor at Walker Road Christian Academy, presents with a shield of scatological humor as cover for unexplained misanthropy.

The principal read him the conclusion:

If no present danger to the school, Mr. Nolting does not seem a likely youth mentor. His controlled hostility is a red flag. He makes no apology for his actions. He approached our inquiry with defiance as a justified skeptic of your academy.

"What would you do if you were me?" the principal asked him.

"Fire me. Safest thing."

It was done. With honest regret, Eric believed, and a fair severance.

"YOU THREW YOUR LIFE UP IN THE AIR to see where you'd land?" a wary Denise asked, and yet she married him.

"Yes," he'd admitted, "but see where I came down?" There was the wild success of *Beyond Logic, Beyond Grammar,* followed by the purchase of the country cottage from which he wooed her. The property, a rural dream, she thought, though surrounded by suburban tracts. It included several unexplored acres of locust and poplar trees with wild shrubbery fighting for a share of sunlight. It was a thick pocket forest with undergrowth of honeysuckle and prickly multiflora, wild grapevines, and Virginia creeper. Here and there a redbud, and dogwood trees were invitations behind the woods' margin.

"Did you wed the place or the man?"

So like her friend Vickie to stick a pin in her marriage. What could she know of Eric's expectant breath, or the wild loss of reason behind his loving eyes?

At the one-man Tyler Agency, Nathan Tyler, smiling, unlocked the glass door himself, all bonhomie for the moment, against the news of no progress, no takers for "The Narcissism of Small Differences." Tyler might have been another therapist, with his self-effacing hesitance, framing and reframing his gently prodding questions. "Who was your imagined editor when you wrote this? Who were your readers?"

The agent didn't say his early enthusiasm had been a mistake, but his lips tightened as he backed toward his desk, and Eric sensed a retreat from the early blessing.

"What if I called it 'The Tyranny of Small Differences'?" he asked.

A short silence was followed by a clearing of two throats.

"You're well positioned for your next, Eric. It would be a shame if we waited too long."

"'The Tyranny of Trivia'?"

"How was your trip? Still using the train?"

"'The Reflexive Contrarian'? I mean, I've thought a lot about the title."

"You've seen what Maggie said?" Tyler handed him a familiar email.

When Maggie Priest said no, the same shadow fell across a dozen desks. In her publishing house were many mansions, a fair share of the respectable imprints in New York. The rest might be told the news at lunch, or know what she said for the asking.

The email said:

Eric Nolting is a wonderful writer. You're fortunate to have him. We waited a long time for this one, and I wanted to like it. But he's written a women's book that women will hate. I have to think the muse of perversity was sitting on his shoulder.

So, not right for us. Better luck with others. And please! Let us see Nolting again.

He glanced at it, and said, "The trip was a nightmare. Denise is barely speaking. I had her in the quiet car, where I could think. Where she wouldn't complain, but one of those so-important businessmen sat down across from us."

"All apped up and floating on his authority?"

"Exactly. With the Raspberry or Blue Fang, all of it."

Eric began to describe the scene in the quiet car. How the man from Trenton disregarded the hissing around him but eventually stood up, looked around, and to no one in particular said, "What?" and "I'm not going anywhere," before sitting again and making another call.

Eric had gotten up in the aisle to glower over him. The

earphone had come off the man as he slid out of reach, toward the window. He remembered the face well enough, the way the nose dived down in a straight line from the forehead, the angle-cut sideburns, and the too-pale eyebrows that seemed the disguise of a dark intention.

The agent, Tyler, found something useful in Eric's New York journey, something to stop his author's anxious hovering over "Narcissism." They parried for half an hour and Eric gave in. He would try to balance the sexual politics in his manuscript, and the title could be changed to the less provocative "Tyranny of Trivia," and Tyler would send it around again. While they waited for acceptance, Eric would start a new book about the man from Trenton and the whole brotherhood of rude Americans.

Down the avenue he went, refreshed, preparing a face for Denise, already eager to be home in Virginia, rearranging the nanogates in his computer, giving form to letters still in the atom's tomb. First the overhaul of "Narcissism." Then all out on "Peacock and Chatterbox: An Epidemic."

The odd thing—though he was anxious to get back and make things better with Denise—when he came to their little hotel, he walked right past. He wanted her to believe in his contrition but couldn't think of words sufficient to the task without giving too much away. He couldn't really tell her, "You know, the book isn't about you. You'd have to be conceited to think so, and you're not conceited."

He made a circuit around the block with nothing settled but a resolve to avoid quarreling, though this might amount to no conversation at all. Under the awning again, he entered the hotel, ready to listen, even to nod, if only to prove his sincerity. He would not argue; silence could speak for demurral.

Denise was not in their room. Eric's computer was on the table, humming softly. It had only to be touched to relight and display the email to her confidante, Vickie— commiserating Vickie in Vermont—who normally joined Denise in audiovisual chat on first Fridays. No question the note, so easily accessed, had been left for him to read.

Vickie dear,

We came to New York so Eric could see Nathan Tyler about the book, plus he's had this idea about a night for us in a small hotel where they put chocolate on the pillows. But he made a scene on the way up. You know how he is around cell phones. (Eric, I know you're reading this.)

He's still got this blood lump on his shin from the lady calling home to ask what she should buy to have with a roast. And right in her ear he said, "You know I like succotash," and she pushed her shopping cart into his leg. He thinks joining an annoying cell phone conversation is the best way to stop it. It was like that with the businessman on the train, only worse. I didn't see it all, but they had to call one of those Homeland soldiers onto the train to sort it out.

I've been looking into this computer while he's off "getting tough with Nathan." The book is worse than I thought. I mean, the thin disguise he puts on me. It amazes me what he thought he could get away with, how the distance he imagined between his keyboard and our world could give him such a foolhardy nerve. The truth is, he needs help, and not just with our marriage. Technology came on too fast for Eric. He hates all these new generations of telemagic. Doesn't know a pad from a podcast and doesn't want to. A wonder he manages his word program.

I won't be staying for the romantic evening he planned. When I sign off here, I'm heading for the station. (The 6:00 P.M., Eric.)

The attachment is "The Narcissism of Small Differences"—his book, the whole thing. Judge for yourself. When you've had enough, maybe you should erase it.

Eric had no intention of chasing after Denise to catch the six o'clock. He'd paid for the room and meant to use it. And what about her nerve, forwarding his unpublished manuscript to Vickie, putting it out there on the wind? Thinking of another reader only magnified his doubt about the book's trivial metaphor, a cone teetering on its point.

How could that compass the marriage, which brushed so resolutely past the grumbling and ill temper, surviving on longevity's inertial guidance? Denise was still attractive to him, with admirable assets under the skin, seductive in ways not visible in a mirror, the more appealing as secrets from herself.

If she criticized his writing, it was only by omission of ready praise, even with the misadventure of the novel, which Nathan could only place with a promise of Eric's next. The most hurtful critic had called him "a doorknob turner who has trouble getting a character from one room to another." Provoked beyond wise silence, he'd written the rebuttal that was sent from a friend's computer: "The reviewer's own fiction is so clouded with omission, one scarcely knows which century we're in, or what continent we're on."

Home again in the Virginia Piedmont, Eric had hardly opened the front door when Denise said, "You left the lights on in the study."

Where to go from there?

His regular retreat was Your Cup in the village a few miles away, where students from the Bible college slung the coffee. Here, behind a newspaper, he could study his American specimens—PTO mothers, pharmaceutical reps, developers, builders, stockbrokers, online students, and businessmen manqué, who made the place their office every day—most all of them chattering as if private matters were the public's concern. When, he wondered, had America lost its modesty?

A letter arrived at the cottage from Amtrak Customer Service, explaining quiet-car policy. It said passengers could not be put off a train for ignoring the "quiet" rule. The railroad was sorry for the unfortunate encounter with traveler Crider on the recent trip to New York, but it was obliged to tell Eric and his wife they were now on the extra-scrutiny list. Addressed to both of them, it was opened by Denise, who wouldn't discuss it, leaving it at full weight on the marriage scales.

Then came an email for Eric from Spideyman@wilddigit:

Did you know that 80 percent of quiet-car passengers have never shushed anyone? And of the remaining 20 percent, half are in favor of disabling a train's automatic announcement system.

Spideyman added his own description of a quiet-car vigilante: "One who rides the train in expectation of pajamas and a pillow." This was followed by a definition of assault: "an intentional act to create apprehension in another of imminent harmful or offensive contact, both a crime and a tort, thus subject to criminal or civil liability. Added physical contact could result in a charge of battery."

If those were the rules, what use Eric insisting, "I never touched him. Maybe his Blue Shark or whatever fell off the man's ear when he ducked away."

"Ducked from what?" Denise asked. "Exactly what happened?"

Eric couldn't say for sure. But he'd lost his balance in the aisle for a moment as the train swayed. He'd fallen toward the man, maybe even touched the ear thing while just grabbing air.

Denise could imagine Eric losing a jury's sympathy, and she chose his moment of shame to confess that Vickie had forwarded "The Narcissism of Small Differences" to their friend Susan. To justify the manuscript's second release, she said Susan might be an arbiter in a way that Vickie—such a close friend—could not.

He had agreed to arbitration?

If Spideyman was Mr. Crider, the man from Trenton, Eric couldn't prove it, but Nathan Tyler said, "Wonderful. Now you've got something to work with. Get going."

Eric couldn't get going. There were more insults from Spideyman, who had discovered the mortgage terms of the Nolting cottage. Nathan offered reassurance: What the internet stole in privacy, it returned in kind. "And by the way, you're not unknown; someone wants to do the cover for 'Narcissism.' How did they hear about it? Never mind, we're not going there."

Still more from Spideyman@wilddigit:

> *Readers can learn more about the writer Eric Nolt-ing in a new contribution to his Wiki Life: "Nolting's* Beyond Logic, Beyond Grammar *has been called 'a condescending plagiarism of other men's mistakes.' For example, he pokes fun at the master storyteller Isaac Singer for writing* egg nest *when he meant* nest egg. *His own attempt at fiction,* The Potter's Odyssey *was described as 'childish in plot and transitions.'"*

Eric was in Your Cup coffee shop, taking notes:

Big Pharma's blondes, glossed lips, black skirts, heels too high for suburban sidewalks, dragging wheeled cases full of adrenaline suppression and erectile encouragement. One of them, on her cell phone, asks a doctor, "Are we on for lunch?"

"Not today," Eric called from his chair. Nathan wanted more involvement from Eric, a running exchange with Spideyman for narrative backbone. As for the "Narcissism" manuscript, the agent offered something he thought would help, but he knew nothing of Denise's reflexive opposition, a contagion, it seemed, when he replied in kind in self-defense—his ability to place blame where it belonged, stolen from him. At the next mention of Tyler's name, Denise left the house. Eric watched her disappear at the edge of the woods.

A restorative walk, she told him when she emerged from the trees at dusk. She'd walked right out of the neighboring development, she said, following the sun west on a back road toward the Blue Ridge. For all the sound of freedom in her unlikely adventure, he doubted Denise had gotten past a kitchen table in the adjacent tract, where a house-husband she knew kept an all-day coffeepot for neighbor-hood women who admired his role reversal. He imagined Denise explaining the futile battle with the man from Trenton, how he had called Spideyman a coward, after which another paragraph was attached to Eric's Wiki Life:

Nolting, fired from the Walker Road Christian Acad-emy in Fairfax, Virginia, broke into the school's com-puter, stealing everything—the personal files of students and patrons, medical and business records.

Denise had hardly finished reading this before look-ing at him and asking, "Are you wearing those clothes into the village?"

"They're right," he said. "I had the whole school in the palm of my hand!"

Denise's mood rhythm was less monthly than seasonal. Like a schoolgirl, she quickened on the first warm days of April, when her down jacket was thrown aside, spring mus-lin barely fell to her knees, and she rattled the whole cottage with the front door as she escaped into the budding world. They were both happier.

That year there was a period of calm before the after-noon he came home to an empty cottage after a session in the coffee shop, where he'd heard the prospect of night lights over youth football praised and damned. Outside, walking along the edge of his backyard, calling into the wall of green, he came on a narrow opening through thorns and low branches. Entering his woods, he was surprised by a worn path leading deeper into his unfamiliar wilderness.

Somewhere close to the center of the small forest he found his wife slouched against the thin trunks of twin dogwood trees. She was smiling under their white canopy, her jersey hanging out of loosened jeans, and garden boots unlaced. Was she lacing or unlacing? He hadn't time to ask before she reached for his hand to draw him down beside her. He had the saving sense not to raise the likelihood of poison ivy as they bruised themselves on the green floor.

Content for the moment, he was buttoning his shirt when she said, "Eric, why don't you just give up?" She wasn't just suggesting the eastern way of ambition denial—but a rebuke in full, and right on the heels of intimacy, like an all-encompassing sigh of dissatisfaction. She meant his writing career, the rejected book, his vigilant detection of social ironies, the absurdity of an eavesdropper's feud with cell phone chatter.

"Not that way, that doesn't go anywhere," she said, tidying herself, getting up to lead him home. Back at the cottage it seemed important to decide which of them had failed to close the kitchen window. They might have shared a quiet dinner, but flies over the food kindled the pressing need to fix blame.

A LETTER ARRIVED FROM LAWYERS FOR Walter Crider, vice president of Stable-Light Equine Therapies, Trenton. A settlement of forty thousand dollars was asked, plus legal fees, to avoid action for assault aboard Amtrak's Northeast

Regional. Another passenger who had witnessed the attack was ready to testify. Agent Nathan called it smoke, but Denise said only Eric and his agent could devise a game in which victory was illusory and penalties real. She started talking to Vickie about going to Vermont for the summer, or until Eric had this under control.

"If you go," he said, "you won't be coming back."

It sounded as much like an ultimatum as a prediction, which frightened both of them into a May of cooperation. They were briefly buoyed by a foreign sale of *Beyond Logic, Beyond Grammar.* And Nathan Tyler had been right about this—What the new age stole in privacy, it repaid in kind. Soiled things were eventually hung out to dry online beside the proud threads. Crider's reprised indignity came into view—three cease and desist orders issued to Stable-Light, citing the man and his associates for unproven claims for their Fingers of Light.

When Eric hesitated it was Nathan who sent Crider a reminder of his reputation, a video of Stable-Light's product in action, a piece of molded plastic with a hand strap and half a dozen rows of light-emitting diodes—steady whites for ordinary soreness, blinking reds and blues for deep-tissue distress. When they all flashed at once, the thing resembled a toy police car on the move as it performed its therapy.

DENISE'S RELEASE OF "The Narcissism of Small Differences" to Vickie had been followed by its transmission to her friend Susan, who sent the manuscript and her sympathy for Denise to her whole address book, and several of these recipients had done the same. Now, by a law of critical mass, the manuscript showed up again in agent Nathan Tyler's email, gathering momentum with a fillip from the post of someone called Piedmont Pocahontas, propelled off the East Coast, through the Cumberland Gap, and over the Continental Divide.

Pocahontas began:

Sisters, in "The Narcissism of Small Differences," a calendar of the quotidian, Eric Nolting, a traveler in a world he never made, has a lover's quarrel with his wife and his society but can't see the betrayal at his own doorstep. You have to pity a heart so eager to disbelieve what the eye can see and the mind should know. Nolting has written a marriage mystery in which the reader is detective, and he a naïf too distracted to explore the secrets of his own domain. Don't grieve for him. He's sitting on a fortune.

A page from the book:

June 20. He stirred and she jumped out of bed to get to the bathroom before him, shut the door, and spoke as if he were standing beside her at the sink—that is, in a voice she knew he couldn't quite hear.

"What?" he called.
"You left the seat up."
"I don't think so."
He heard the seat fall.
"Well, it's wet!" she said.
"How could it be wet if it was up?"

Downstairs, he made coffee and toast for her. She discovered crumbs in the marmalade.

Eric went upstairs to dress, and when he came down, she was halfway out the door for one of her neighborhood strolls, maybe with a stop in the woods under the dogwood bower. She told him the seat could be up and be wet, too, and cargo pockets were for people half his age.

At Your Cup, he was sitting next to a table of reborn theologians discussing atheism's perversity in the face of such overwhelming evidence. "It takes fifty-seven chemical agents to make blood clot. Can you imagine not understanding it would take a creator to accomplish this?"

The speaker might as well have been asking Eric, who couldn't hold his tongue. "Why use fifty-seven when he could use just one?"

Agent Nathan asked him, "What's going on? Are we giving your book away? How do all these people know about it?"

Without Eric's approval, Nathan had sent a friend in Trenton to have a look at the Stable-Light factory, the reclaimed ground floor of the warehouse. Doors were locked, but through a broken window he saw seven men and women with soldering irons, chattering in Spanish around a table covered with wires and plastic.

Denise, who had moved into the guest room for a week, agreed to come back to the marriage bed if he would respect her she-time in their little forest. Was it his skewed perception, or was she instigator and winner by default of all petty quibble? If she said, "Maine residents don't like summer people," and he said, "They depend on them," and she said, "No, I wont go there anymore," his silence would be a surrender meant to end the discussion of their next vacation. If he said a model in a catalog looked like Winona Ryder, and she said, "Not a bit; look, the jaw is all wrong," should he give up before she went looking for another magazine to prove she was right?

SPIDEYMAN HAD LET ERIC KNOW that friends in Bayonne who usually keep their road travel behind tinted glass on the northern end of the Jersey Turnpike also knew the way south, over the Delaware and Potomac Rivers, with a dashboard screen that could light the path to Eric's mortgaged cottage in Virginia.

When it came, the car from New Jersey was long and gunmetal gray, with two men in front and one in back. Eric, at the end of his driveway, saw them cruise by slowly for a brazen inspection. The two in front were wearing ties crossed over in a knot's first position, well below the collar. Was this because completed four-in-hands were for wusses, or a measure of their disdain for the insulting landscape, where a single cottage had its own forest?

Instead of warning Denise about their visitors from the north, he said, "All right, what if I do give up?" He'd withdraw the book, break with his agent, maybe substitute teach while he studied for the degree required to work full-time in the county system.

"Now? At your age?" And after a silence, "What did you expect me to say?"

THROUGH THE KITCHEN WINDOW he could see her look side to side and behind her before pulling a branch aside and stepping into the woods. He smashed a glass into shards against the sink. He sat to sulk before rousing himself.

"No more of this."

He should have put on heavier pants to follow her through the thorns. Hard to believe she could slip through here in shorts and sandals. The narrow line of worn earth he followed was only a partial secret under its leafy cover.

He didn't whistle well, so he clambered through a thicket, coughing and clearing his throat as he approached the dogwood shrine. He heard "Oh hell" before seeing her pale back, retreating, following behind the bare-shouldered man. Clothes in hand, they were running toward the other side of the little wilderness. Eric went stumbling back toward the house. More surprised by the betrayal or his sudden sense of freedom? He wasn't sure which.

On the phone she said she wasn't coming back, didn't want anything in the cottage, no clothes, nothing to remind her of her life there. This was only honored till the next afternoon, when she returned for her toilet kit. And the Mumby print. And a lamp. Well, a few clothes till Monday, when this man was taking her shopping—in particular, a dress her niece had made for her. And a pair of shoes you couldn't get anymore. Actually, all her shoes. And a side table that had been in her family and might be valuable. Before she left, the back of her lover's station wagon was full.

As she walked out, Eric ducked away from the feint of her lips toward his cheek. He saw the wistful way she looked behind her at the house—financial remorse or sentimental pang? He saw a little girl in the backseat of the wagon, staring daggers. Denise turned back and sat down on the front step of the cottage for a moment, patting the slate beside her for him. He wouldn't sit. She got up and was on her way, gone for good.

She could, and eventually would, say he might have salvaged the marriage simply by sitting down at that moment and talking to her. She would have told him about the other man's quick temper and his daughter's passive aggression.

So Denise was not there when the call came from Nathan Tyler about Maggie Priest's change of heart, the apology for a too-hasty rejection of "The Narcissism of Small Differences." Its viral journey had propelled it past her indifference. Tyler said another imprint in Maggie's own house was bidding against her, and a third editor had called, making both their offers look very stingy. Nathan was preparing for an auction.

Denise was not there to ponder the multiplication she'd set in motion with her first transmission of the manuscript. Within the year, she had retreated to Vickie in Vermont, and wasn't around to see their little wilderness transformed with a share of his new prosperity into parkland, opened to the community of tract houses where her affair with the woods satyr had begun, blossomed, and died in less than a butterfly's span.

In Vermont, she did not hear about it when violence arrived at the cottage. If Eric had been truly afraid, he might have stood to the side when he drew curtains across the windows or varied his routine, or at least performed it before dark, when his figure was not so clearly backlit by living room lamps.

Denise, several affairs and another marriage later, leafing through a celebrity magazine, saw Eric in a double-breasted black jacket—"An Author Takes His Medals." What medals? Behind eye patch and black band angling across his cheek. She transformed him in her memory from dreamer to poser before she read, "blinded in one eye by a shotgun fired through the glass door of his Virginia home."

Goodness.

Eric regretted having submitted himself to that magazine of clothes and chitchat. He couldn't avoid their camera, but he shouldn't have accepted the Italian suit they provided for the banquet. Patiently answering silly questions only made him look stupid.

This was the first time he'd heard from Denise since she'd received her share of his new wealth. The early marriage in Virginia did not weigh heavy on her memory.

"What's the story? People know who you are? You got shot?"

No remorse in her volley of surprise.

"Did you settle up with that man who fixes horses with Christmas lights? Who dressed you in those pants? Were you going wading?"

In less than a minute he was at the impasse of old when, if silence is aggression, civil response may be admission of defeat.

"Listen, Eric." She'd read an article about cell phone irritation. It was all about hearing just one side of a conversation. "Are you there?"

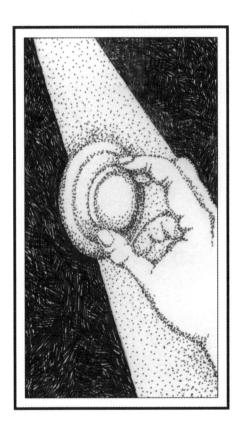

Wax on, wax off, all she'd need to know.

THE VOICE OF THE VALLEY

Gwen, reduced to ash in a celadon urn, sat on a low table in the middle of the Meeting House. The pews were not quite full, though the Quakers were good about this sort of thing, opening their doors and hearts, even to a mischievous soul like Gwen. Since Gwen was from England, with no family in America, and no affiliation with a church, someone had to arrange a funeral for her. So Brenda, who knew her better than most, had asked the Cross Creek Meeting to host the farewell.

Behind Gwen's back, but with some affection, Brenda and others whose lives she'd touched had called her "Nothing Left Over." Five feet tall, and nothing left over. When she bought the little AM radio station in Point of Rocks, she had nothing left over to run it. If she splurged on a restaurant meal, there might be nothing left over for the tip. Now, turned to dust, she had nothing left over for her urn's burial.

In death as in life, others made up for Gwen's shortfall. Her bank took the radio station, covered final bills, and paid for the cremation. Brenda made a contribution to the Meeting as dues for a respectable farewell to the woman who'd given her a job. And the Quakers provided a small plot for interment of the urn.

Brenda began the ceremony by reading from a brief vita—Gwen's British birth, a hardscrabble youth, an early interest in radio, her journey to Virginia, and American citizenship, followed by her gamble on the little AM station on the Maryland side of the Potomac River. "Then this."

The reading came to an abrupt end, to the embolism that killed her. With no clergy between this minimal goodbye and the urn's burial, Brenda feared a service so brief, it might embarrass the gracious Quakers, who might wonder if there were any sincere mourners among the visitors.

After an unconscionably long silence, she rose again, fairly begging the little gathering for reminiscence. The empty minute that followed had the air of group refusal before one of Gwen's acquaintances stood to plead for honesty: "Let's not pretend she's on her way to a mansion in the sky." It would be wrong, he said, to impute a formal faith where none existed. Anyway, she'd be uncomfortable anywhere the pipes were reliable and the linoleum flat.

Scripture and resurrection were outflanked for the moment by this man, who said Gwen believed it was stories that were eternal, not the body or the soul. This loosened the collective tongue, and tales of the Englishwoman led up and down the river valley from one town to another.

A used-car salesman from Point of Rocks told how Gwen would invite herself to dinner, and not leave until he'd bought another spot on her station. A lady from Lucketts said she gave Gwen a car in return for promotion of her cut-flower business, a clunker serviced and gassed in return for a Brunswick filling station's commercials.

Yes, her Leesburg tax adviser said, she was a creative bookkeeper; he meant her returns were full of holes where numbers belonged, all lacy with barter; that she'd been more gypsy than businesswoman. There was a moment of laughter in the room, and now a sense that people were there to amuse and be amused as much as to mourn. The woman beside Brenda was whispering to her: "She used us like a lurcher, to plunder where she wouldn't go herself."

A man from Neersville, maybe sensing a loss of decorum, began to read from the dictionary in his hand: "'*Embolus*. From the Greek. Days inserted to bring the calendar into balance with the solar year. In the eighteenth century, it was used to mean the insertion of foreign or absurd matter.' That's what we had here," he went on, "an absurd bit of matter that got into her head."

An elder, restive on the facing bench, had heard enough. "Without faith," he said, "we commit to an eternal nightmare."

From the back of the meeting: "I didn't say she believed in nothing. I said she had no formal faith." Brenda, responsible for the ashes and their retinue, stood for a third time. Wanting to apologize to the hosting Quakers, she plunged into an unrehearsed version of Gwen.

In the beginning, she said, was the untroubled air over Point of Rocks. Then WPOR was born, 1320 AM. With a weak vital sign, 500 watts, sunrise to sunset. The signal from its short tower barely reached a three-mile radius. Gwen bought the frail station from a failing owner for the promise to pay his creditors, then went knocking on doors for investment in her new Voice of the Valley.

She'd worked briefly as a producer for BBC Radio in Washington. Diving headfirst into business, she was both ambitious and needy. Gwen had come to these river towns at the Virginia-Maryland border to give open mike to all the people—local poets, musicians, gospel singers, small businessmen, developers, preservationists, and preachers, not to forget an Albanian with a Balkan grievance or a booster of Heifer International. Any who'd speak or perform without pay.

She let Brenda, a DJ wannabe, do a three-hour show on Sundays. No salary, just on-the-job training. Gwen asked for a learning fee, whatever Brenda could afford. Nothing. "Come in next Sunday," Gwen told her. "Bring your own music." Brenda's records, a shelf of vinyl, twit-written novelty tunes of the post–World War II decades, and sappy crooners, fit for the station's two aging turntables, most of them voices Gwen hoped the music-rights people might have forgotten about.

When a record was finished, Brenda turned a knob to the left. Ready to talk, she turned another to the right. "Wax on, wax off. That's all you need to know," she was told. Soon enough, she was the station's principal DJ and host, working five hours a day for less than minimum wage in the months Gwen could afford it. "You're the voice of the valley," she was told. "What more could you want?"

The eulogy was blowing itself off course again. Brenda's next thought was, "No country! No hillbilly music!" Without context, it left the gathering confused, but the words, which were posted on soundproof glass for everyone who worked behind Gwen's microphone, led Brenda onto another path, and more secure footing.

WPOR, she explained, had a forbidden library of old 78 rpm records—the famous vocalists of Nashville, left by the station's first owners. Gwen despised their whiny

sentiment but hoped there'd be antique value in the collection someday. Recalling this and that about her thrifty
employer, depending on Gwen's history to find its own
way, Brenda moved left, right, and forward, as if trusting
another rock to be there as she jumped across a river, too
involved in maintaining her balance to keep an eye on the
danger ahead, which was a veer off course to the deceased's
miserable childhood in Widnes on the Mersey.

Brenda asked the gathering to imagine the young
Gwen under a river bridge, at the mercy of some thuggish
boys she'd provoked, and later wading into the rising river
to save one of her antagonists from drowning. Too many
fathers had passed through Gwen's house, none of them
hers. At ten years old, she cooked and did the shopping.
Franks and cabbage. In her teens there was a thing she'd
do at sing-alongs in the pub, which brought the constable
around to their door on Monday mornings for a chat with
her mother. Eventually it was up by her own straps to a
redbrick education, where she found her . . .

At a loss again, Brenda grabbed the next thing to mind.
"She wasn't afraid of death. I can tell you that." She didn't
say what Gwen had actually told her: "I want to go while
my tits are still good." Brenda had known other British
women like her, proud and forward with their bosoms.
"Twin conic," the sometime station engineer had observed,
"forced to the shape by the harness," his randy tongue
licensed by his negligible salary, though he knew less about
Gwen's naked shape than a valley high school boy.

Now Brenda described a woman still fresh at forty-two,
with thick, dark hair, and a mouth that closed sweetly over
English teeth, never straightened. An open face—she

couldn't really say guileless, but there was never a mask on the nervy presumption, Gwen's expectation of community sacrifice to the people's voice, her "radio-free Catoctin." Her business plan was blather and smile.

There was an FCC inspector's visit when the intern failed to perform with coffee and doughnuts. In a childish pet, maybe ashamed of what had happened or what she'd said in a back room to bring mercy on her weakling signal, her spotty program logs, her ignorance of the emergency broadcast procedure, her absent engineer. There was no fine, no warning; rather, the next week, a form to be filled with grand numbers, not a punishment, but a prize.

There was Gwen transformed, no longer angry, waving the papers that allowed an increase in signal strength to 10,000 watts, doing a pirouette, arms extended as over a grand new circle of radiated power; her Voice of the Valley might soon reach forty thousand homes, all the way into Leesburg.

WITH THE NEW POWER CAME a new restriction. A thirty-degree cone to be carved out of the signal in the direction of Baltimore to avoid interference with a city station, a new challenge for her engineer. To be certain their listening area was duly shaped, he and Gwen would set off each evening to take the station's new pulse. One hundred and thirty-five locations to be tested on concentric circles, reaching out twenty miles from their tower.

Using borrowed field meters, they were trying to complete the job in the one-month period they were allowed to broadcast until midnight. Brenda, left alone in the studio when evening fell, spun something soft, wondering if Gwen and the engineer could hear it. With the moon rising over the Potomac, she sent Sinatra floating down the river, doing it Gwen's way.

A WOMAN WAS PHONING THE STATION. She was screaming, "My son's gone. He just started high school. He's gone! Get off the line!" She had tried to call the police, but all she could hear on her phone was WPOR—Frank Sinatra and Brenda. Her Bobby had just lost his girlfriend. She thought he might destroy himself. "Get off the line! You're in the telephone!"

Brenda could hear it on her end now, Sinatra backing up the frantic woman. Lights were flashing on the other phone: "What the hell are you people doing?" WPOR was cross-talking all over the valley, with Gwen out there somewhere in the dark, testing their rogue signal, her cell phone not answering.

Gulping air in the Meeting House, Brenda sensed her account of Gwen was drawing too much attention to herself, but there was no going backward from the place where she'd used the one sure way to get Gwen's attention—spinning one of the whiny voices, Ernest Tubb "walking the dog," with the billy bleat that would curl Gwen's hair. In less than a minute she'd taken the bait.

"What are you doing?" Firing and rehiring Brenda in a breath. She said, "Look, don't go off the air. We're almost finished." It didn't seem to matter about the boy or that their signal was in the phone lines.

"Picture the boy," Brenda said. "Not yet fifteen, in his

baseball hat, brim backward, making his way down the Potomac bank after dark, taking a few slogging steps in the shallows and climbing onto a flat boulder, saying his farewell to the world, looking through the clear water in the moonlight, down to the slippery rocks at the bottom, wondering if the current would be strong enough to carry him away."

"I'm coming." He spoke to the middle of the river, as if the girl was out there, the one who wouldn't answer his eyes in the school hallway. He heard his name, a question. "Bobby?" A woman was climbing onto the rock beside him. "Look down there," she said, her blouse hanging out of her jeans. A finger pointed beyond her painted toenails. His eyes followed downward to a flashing pattern in the water, a school of carp streaking past, two hundred or more, all of a size, foot-long missiles on some downstream mission.

"If you're in the water with them, they won't touch you," she said. "You could be made of stone." And the fish were gone as suddenly as they'd arrived. He took a step closer to the edge.

"Wait," she said, "I'm coming, too."

"What are you doing? How do you know my name?"

"No need to get our clothes wet," she said.

Her arms rose over her head, lifting her shirt, and then her hands were sliding down her hips as she bent over, sliding out of her jeans and panties. She moved up beside him, as if unaware her naked confidence could reveal all the sorry insufficiencies of the girl who spurned him. Stepping out of her sandals, too, she led the boy by the hand into the river.

The water was quickly up to her chin, and he said what he might have said to any girl in the river, holding his hand. "Do you want to get your hair wet?" with all that implied about life after the river, no more or less than "Shall we go back?"

Brenda has Gwen on the rock once more, where she's using her clothes as a towel, the dripping hair between her legs beginning to curl again, and glossy skin turning back to matte, saying, "Come on. Your mother's worried."

Brenda was still jumping from stone to stone, sometimes surprised by her landing places, but reminding her listeners it wasn't the boy, it was Gwen's memory she was trying to deliver safely to the other side.

Her first question for Gwen had been the same as the boy's. How did she know Bobby would be at the river, or even how to recognize him?

Hadn't she grown up at Widnes on the Mersey? As a child she'd stood under the Runcorn bridge more than once, asking the current to deliver her into the Irish Sea.

The police and family, too, had looked for Bobby by the Potomac, but in too much of a hurry. They hadn't the conviction to walk upstream and under the bridge, first refuge of the forlorn in any river town.

Afterward, Brenda had gone to examine the place for herself. The scene of Bobby's deliverance under the moon was, by daylight, a collage of vulgar celebration, pocked mud cracking in the sun, overflown by bluebottles and mosquitoes. There were twisted beer cans, broken liquor bottles, a yellowed sheath, caught on a twig, tumescent again in the current. Acrid air hung over the pissed-on remains of a driftwood fire where a plastic diaper uncurled. No angels here.

Only the high-water mark of the cleansing river offered

hope in a place that could be a fugitive's retreat on either side of the ocean. There had been no doubt in Gwen's mind about that. It was the first place she looked, her own redemption the furthest thing from her mind, unaware a clot was already forming, preparing a farewell ceremony of its own on the shore of an artery, waiting to cast off into the channel with no one to charm it back. No idea that she might need assistance, too, crossing to the other shore.

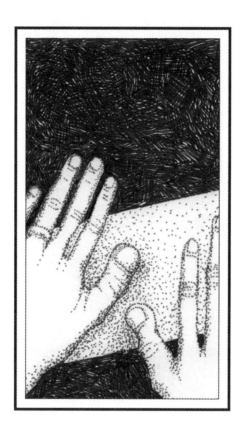

Thumbs like parking meters.

FAMILIARS

O<small>NCE AGAIN</small> J<small>EFF AND HIS WIFE</small>, L<small>AURIE</small>, with Mattie and her husband, Daniel, were driving down to the coastal house they'd rented together for seventeen consecutive summers—a record maybe for two-couple compatibility.

Known to the four as "the Camel," the two-level beach house, raised on stilts in the North Carolina sand, was as mismatched in its seaside row as the motley of furniture within— sleigh bed, brass bed, Empire sofa, Morris chair, pressed-oak dining set. The heavier furniture and kitchen appliances had worn dark depressions in the original linoleum.

Ungainly on the outside, the house was as easy to slip into as an old shoe. It greeted them again with the familiar message painted on the frame of the entrance hall mirror: "Deep in the gleaming glass, she sees all past things pass." And after seventeen summers, Margaret, the agent who managed the rental, had become "Peggy dear," the one who made sure the Camel was available for their August fortnight. Having dealt with the pre-vacation arrangements seventeen times over, she kept the couples properly in order with a memory aid: "Jeff and Laurie, hunky-dory; Daniel and Mattie, he's her fatty," though you'd hardly call Daniel fat.

Observing them on vacation for the first time, you might be thrown off by the indiscriminate teasing and flirtation, though not if you knew their history. Bonded since university days, they'd lived in an off-campus house in 1980s Ann Arbor. In that time of backward-gazing envy at the guilt-free wandering of the previous decade, they had even swapped partners for a season. But with the real world looming in the weeks before graduation, they had returned to the original pairing. It wasn't long after that, they settled into their conventional marriages.

The four remained close, with a lasting pride in the peaceful way they absorbed the bruises of their early ménage. The two couples lived in a northern Virginia county, where Jeff was a headhunter for civilian cybersecurity hires in the Defense Department, and Daniel, a systems engineer in corporate computing. Mattie designed a wool company's most intricate knitting patterns, while Laurie's preoccupation was her journal writing, which reached back to their time in Ann Arbor. It gratified her to see how the mundane jotting gained significance with age.

Of the four, only Mattie, the knitter, had shown resistance to another summer reunion, an inward groan at the prospect, and a shrug when husband Daniel reminded her of the August dates. "What?" he'd asked her. And louder: "What?" It was nothing, she assured him, just all the deferred obligations, and September always rushing toward them.

In truth, Mattie enjoyed the summer gatherings as much as any of them. But she was thinking of Laurie's notebook, her pen so busy in the evenings, the curiosity and cryptic scribbling. What if Laurie became tired of anonymity and released her privileged note taking to a wider world? And Mattie disliked being thought of as a woman of leisure. She still had something to prove, if only to parents whose faith in her university education had been shaken by a daughter whose career rested on the manipulation of knitting needles.

With the vacation upon them, Mattie apologized for her moody resistance. Her commitment to the four-way friendship ran deeper than her fear. If Laurie's busy pen unnerved her, or her husband's walks down the beach with Laurie seemed overlong, these reactions must be her own communal failing. It would have calmed her further to know how many times "Mattie's guilelessness" was celebrated in the journal, which was kept with a mariner's strict rule for his ship's log; nothing could be erased, only amplified. Without that rule, Laurie might have forgotten things like "Couldn't blame Mattie for any of today's fuss." Whatever the fuss was had been lost, but not Laurie's written declaration of it.

The two couples had produced three children. There was Jeff and Laurie's twenty-year-old Charlotte, who was taking a college gap year. Squandering the gap, they thought, in a local coffee shop. To either side of Charlotte in age were Mattie and Daniel's boys, Gerald, twenty-three, who had breezed through college, and their less ambitious Rudy, eighteen, enrolled after high school in a music theory course at their community college, and living with his guitar in their basement.

Forced together over the years, the children's regard for one another was warm and cool by turns, the older Gerald's early attraction to Charlotte worn away by the embarrassments of puberty and forced proximity. The summer vacations, the Thanksgivings, the Christmas meals had made her more a sister, a difficult one, mirror-proud, he thought. Before the vacation this year, Charlotte had texted him, "If y're still Gerry7@plenty.net, pls respond abt 'rents to N.C. again." At twenty, she was thoroughly tired of the too-enthusiastic togetherness of the four parents, their tiresome displays of mutual admiration. Gerald did not reply.

The women, Mattie and Laurie, were used to indulging their husbands' mutual commiseration, their *mal de cybersiècle*. Both men knew the paths to their computers' inner lives, how to reach and read screens of arcane code. But for all their computer savvy, they acted as if they stood alone in sensitivity to IT's spawn—that cloud of information hanging over the planet. They were trapped under that roof of open secrets. Tied to the same generation of phones, tablets, laptops, their lives bared to the datamining engineers, the masters of surveillance capitalism. The planet-heating cover was as insidious to them as the carbon wrapping the globe.

They watched in pain while others no brainier than they turned wide swaths of this cover into personal fortunes. They strolled the beach while their wives took to hands and knees in the sand, searching for sharks' teeth, happily apart from their husbands' latest sorrows. Such a circus on the internet, the men agreed, and a circus had its amusements: Jeff's news from frozen Archangel by way of New York: "Hello, do you remember? You could not see me. I am Marina with Russia. Waiting for you in New York. See my picture. Are you sorry for the hair on my eye?"

Daniel coincidentally had just been contacted by another Russian lady, Anna, age twenty-six, looking for a friendship, maybe more. "Call to me," with international digits provided, though Anna's picture was no match for the swim-suited Marina on Jeff's phone. "Did you get this?" Daniel pulled up a late message of financial opportunity: "Revealed. The first energy generator that violates laws of physics, humiliating top scientists. Even after eighty-four years."

The men saw no irony in the skin-close proximity of their nth-generation cell phones tucked in the pockets of their bathing trunks. Cooling their feet in the ocean, they shared more symmetry: mutual reports of stranded familiars, Jeff's friend Amos in the Cairo airport, and Daniel's cousin in a police station in Amsterdam, their wallets and passports stolen, with no recourse but the kindness of contacts in America. And, as if reducing their pair of virtual obligations to an easy solution, both men had been contacted by a potential benefactor, Fred Ugwu, officer of a bank in Burkina Faso, ready to pay 40 percent of the principal for help in transferring $10.5 million dormant in the account of a deceased depositor.

They could be thankful the digital intrusions had left something of their privacy intact, things the data cloud could never capture, traits and habits, endearing or off-putting, which had attracted, split, and recombined the two couples twenty years earlier, quirks and endearments still at play, along with others since acquired and observed:

Daniel's bitten-to-nub fingernails, his apnea and recently acquired night-breathing apparatus, once attached, making sex a bridge too far; his wet-eyed emotion in poetic recitation, the accuracy of his impromptu imitations, his one dance move, with his arm pumping up and down like an oil rig.

Mattie's spatulate thumbs, her snorting laugh, which no amount of Daniel's imitation could discourage, that beautiful face belying the comic explosion from her perfectly formed nose, the ever-so-gentle touch of her loving hand, one dimpled cheek, her tiresome, nettling skepticism: "Interesting—if true."

Jeff's slight lisp, like a radio newsman's, noticeable enough to make him want to prove it no impediment at all, really a complement to his measured conversation; his heavy beard, face dark by early afternoon, his inclusive kindness, his lightly worn political acumen, the humorous confusion of his legs on water skis; his persistent "hopefully" habit.

Laurie's tendency to leap to a contrary position; the wide birthmark on her cheek, which Jeff called "love paint," never covered with makeup, her bright, perfectly spaced teeth, a tongue that could be flexed into clover shape, a pleasing singing voice, garrulous in a checkout line. Alone among the four, she talked in that millennial pattern that turned all declarations into questions.

All the stuff of endearment or repulsion inscribed in longevity's permanent ink. At someone's house party in a long-ago winter in Ann Arbor, Jeff and Daniel had stood looking across a room at Jeff's then partner, Mattie, standing with some younger boys, when Daniel said, "Will you look at our high-bush, low-ass lady," waiting for a laugh. Jeff flinched at the accuracy of it, the backward tilt and tipped-up pelvis, as if Mattie imagined herself at a fancier do, holding a posture of impregnability. Harsh for all its descriptive acuity.

It wasn't revenge so much as equalizing banter when Jeff, on his way to class with Mattie, came up behind Daniel and asked her, "Was he always a toe walker?"

Daniel? A toe walker? Mattie wasn't familiar with the term, but Daniel did spring up a bit when he walked, bouncing forward on the balls of his feet. In the library next day, she learned that toe walking could be a symptom of autism in toddlers, and sometimes a sign of aggression in older children and adults. But there was little aggression in Daniel, or any of them.

In their Ann Arbor cohabitation, the four had taken turns cooking, washing up, and doing housecleaning. You'd hardly know they were students under academic pressure. No beer-sticky floors. In this respect, the women agreed, they might be self-denied prisoners of habit. Their revolt was that interim of switched intimacy. Looking backward, they considered the peaceful transitions a proof of the maturity that had followed them into adult lives. The men liked to think it had been their idea. They were wrong.

They'd been sitting around their dining table, finishing off a bottle of that strawberry-flavored booze water called Boone's Farm, when Jeff said, "Everybody's hands on the table, palms down." Mattie hesitated, guessing what was coming, though she obliged. Right away, all eyes on her thumbs. "Parking meters!" Jeff exploded. And Mattie laughed with the others because her thumbs were surely oddities. But weren't all of them freaks of one kind or another? From hilarity to sober discussion; it was Laurie who said, "Mattie and I have been thinking? We're all in a kind of rut."

No betrayal, the switch was raised for debate by

Laurie, and discussed almost clinically. They might have been having a house meeting about the chore schedule. To accommodate Mattie, Jeff would take on contraceptive responsibility and drop a morning seminar—he didn't need the credits—to match Mattie's no-class schedule on Friday. Mattie's foam mattress only fit the bed she'd been sleeping in, so the men would shift rooms, Daniel accepting half the closet space he'd been used to.

The same four-way peace carried on. It was only in the bedrooms they went to each night that you'd notice the difference. It had been the university housing office that brought the compatible foursome together, and it took little time for this default menagerie to form a discrete cell, walled off from encroachment of the wider student community. In that era of venereal fright, long before an epidemic made pod life a thing of necessity. In their closed foursome, there was no fear in recombining as Laurie-Daniel and Mattie-Jeff.

The four had been the more compatible for their inherited freedom from dogma. Daniel's parents had neither hidden their Jewish heritage nor kept its rituals. Laurie's bloodline included a great-uncle who'd written *The Mistakes of Jesus*, and a mother guided by Emerson's "Self-Reliance"; Jeff's Quaker parents had produced a nonjudgmental son, while Mattie had faced down and overcome her family's fear that liberal arts were a pathway to artisanal poverty.

At the beach, while the two couples relaxed into vacation freedom, Jeff and Laurie's daughter, Charlotte, spent carefree mornings in her Leesburg coffee shop, chatting with regulars, her phone on the table, ready for calls from "rents on the Outer Banks." Unlike her father, she felt cozily wrapped in the information surround, mindless of the young man across from her, typing her conversations into his blog, "Coffee-Shop Diary," building a small but growing audience for her mother's recycled beach news. Without scruple to privacy, Charlotte's voice competed in the coffee shop with the transatlantic exuberance of a German au pair Skyping daily with a sister in Frankfurt.

"All of them in the same beach house again," Charlotte complained, "I think it's pervy."

On the Carolina coast, beyond the sliding glass doors of the Camel's dining room, the sea at sunset gave majesty to "remember whens," and old news that could only interest those four alone, reminiscences brought forward and released as calmly as the in and out of the lapping tide.

"He didn't!"

"He did, you know."

Any embarrassment quickly ebbed into silence. In fact, this year the four made a circle of satisfaction in one another's accomplishments—the award Mattie was getting for invention of a kind of knitting on top of knitting, relief sculpture in wool. She was "Ninja Knit" to an internet community dazzled by the work. Jeff was about to be made the headhunters' managing partner, with a commensurate income bump. Daniel was already his company's indispensable *genius domus* in software crises. And who could tell; there was the tacit possibility that under Laurie's vigilant eye they might come forth one day as the disguised celebrities of an anonymous beach house chronicle.

"Look at this." Daniel was showing them pictures of his wife's latest creation captured in his cell phone, a woolen landscape in relief, with a red machine laying down a swath of wheat on a rolling field. The post was followed by:

"Someone take credit for this."

"How does she do it?"

"She?"

"All right, he/she. Amazing either way."

"The thread continues? Ha-ha."

"Yarn?" asked Daniel.

"Oh be quiet," Mattie hissed. "I asked you not to share that."

Thanks to Charlotte's loose lips and the "Coffee-Shop Diary" entries, the "ménage à quatre" in North Carolina had taken up residence in the cybersphere. The seventeenth reunion of two couples and a speculation of crawling at night or perhaps assignations in the sedge. Charlotte's account passed on in Billy's blog recounted a Russian sex talker's invitation on a father's cell phone.

Up north, Charlotte sent another text to Gerald. "I kn yr getting ths. We ned to tlk."

This time Gerald replied. "Haven't you already been talking too much?"

"Are you aware of what's going on down there?"

"That your mother thinks she's on a private beach?"

"You could tell your father to lift his eyes."

"Shy rights for the topless?"

"Be civil. We have a problem."

"Like the last time we were down there? You slapped me. Remember?"

"I was thirteen!"

"Sixteen and thirteen? Isn't that about right?"

From cyber thrust and parry to truce, Charlotte and Gerald agreed to meet in the coffee shop.

WITH BILLY'S COFFEE-SHOP BLOG circulating further, not just Laurie but the whole beach party was aware of their new unwanted celebrity. They put themselves on communication lockdown.

The women's collection of sharks' teeth grew to two dozen. The daily hunt was more fun than the jigsaw puzzle of a lighthouse. Fossilized teeth from sixty million years ago gave the hunt a timeless excitement, while the men had nothing as interesting to show for their two weeks, just darkened tan lines above and below their trunks. Wistful as they strolled. No matter how sunny, always under the data cloud, their musing drifting away on the breeze.

On the last night of the vacation, the four drank a good deal of gin before dinner, but you wouldn't blame alcohol for what happened. In lubricated camaraderie, old affectation unremarked: Mattie's provocative party posture, unchanged since university; the way Daniel bounced into the room—ready to pounce on what? They were all seated around the coffee table, watching a cloche bonnet grow from two balls of wool, fixed on the rapid click of Mattie's knitting needles. Her fingers slowed or hurried ahead with the pace of the conversation and Jeff's recollection of the heroic toss of a basketball from half-court. Her hands came to a full stop.

"Interesting—if true," she said.

Daniel's eyes rolled up toward the ceiling. "Do you have to doubt everything?"

Her fingers began to move again. God, it's aggravating, he thought, reminding everyone in the room of her industry while they chatted about nothing important. He snapped.

"Damn it! Could you stop with the click-click!"

Silence. Up to him to repair the moment. Instead, he said, "Come off your high horse, Mattie. It's no mystery, what you do. It's just knit or purl. Binary. You're as digital as the rest of us." There was silence again, then his merriment standby: "All hands on the table, palms down."

Quick as slapjack, Mattie yanked a needle from her work, spilling a row of stitches, and stabbed the needle full force into the back of her husband's hand, past tendon and bone, all the way into the table. The four of them stared at the little circle of blood spreading over the wound.

INSTEAD OF SHOUTING and a vacation gone haywire, the silence turned into a panicky four-way push for repair. Laurie grabbed the car keys to drive Daniel to Emergency Care. She thought inexpert removal of the needle could do further damage, but Daniel had already pulled it free, and Mattie was wrapping the wound with a dish towel. It was agreed that Jeff would stay behind to talk Mattie down from a confused self-dread and a sudden palsy in the hand that had stabbed her husband.

The Emergency Care people, awakened by the night

bell, wanted first to know how this happened, and were insulted to be told it was an accident. They kept accusing eyes on Laurie. There was an aside to Daniel as a tetanus shot was given: "I'm calling the police," and the medical tech would have done it if Daniel hadn't insisted he couldn't charge anyone for his own carelessness.

On the way home, he was sitting sideways in the front seat, staring in grateful wonder at his driver.

"What?" Laurie said.

"This," he said, touching the birthmark on her cheek. As if a once ragged continent had become a charmed island, offering succor to a mutineer's shame.

At the cottage, the two others were chatting behind a closed bedroom door. Easy conversation and occasional laughter. Laurie and Daniel nodded in silent approval of the other couple's privacy. They poured the last of the gin over ice, kicked back in the living room, ready to let their mates choose their own curfew, giving themselves over to confessions of old prejudices and desires.

More time passed and eventually they understood that Jeff and Mattie were not coming out to join them. Laurie tried their door. It was locked. Her pursed lips and Daniel's raised brow were less the signals of resignation than first signs of mutual satisfaction in the night's new freedom. They went hand in hand into the other bedroom and began to talk about how they would do this, with a gentleness and memories of each other's expectations.

By morning, all were in their own rooms again. At nine, there was bleary-eyed humming in the kitchen. The first question was, "Which line in the percolator?" And the first quibble, which of two routes north they should take.

They were out of state before eleven, with a succession of public radio stations doing most of the talking, and little thought of home-front damage or confused children or office colleagues, though Laurie said, "Thank God none of us uses social media," to which the men might have piped together, "No, they use us."

Behind them, the Camel waited by the lapping tide.

"You have to have a little courage," she said,
squeezing his hand.

IN THE TIME OF MAGIC

"You're on a short leash, young man. I'll be watching you." The dean reinstating him looked up from his desk with squint-eyed suspicion. "Keep the social blinders on."

Fair enough. Five gap years was a long absence for a returning scholar. In 1972, his first year in Charlottesville, Michael had been linked to one of the university's Gypsy scholars, but his abrupt departure had as much to do with his introduction to Kepler's laws in freshman physics—the God-like simplicity of planetary motion jolting him from the certainty of his atheistic orbit around the sun. Then the enchantments of a young lady of the town, Nadine, a daughter of Aquarius who took him spinning across the continent toward California.

At the time there'd been a band of young men and women using the university as their athletic club with scholastic benefit. Shock troops of "a revolution," they poached on the campus and its amenities from a communal house on the edge of town. Some had forged ID cards, others used friends in the student community for cover.

They played on the tennis courts, swam in the pool, used exercise machines and shower rooms, even ate in the cafeteria. One of them had used Michael as a chatting classmate, slipping into lecture halls beside him. Michael followed him one evening back to their safe house. He heard the residents singing a mockery of the university's anthem around a basement keg, and met the teenage lady Nadine, who led him west, away from books and his late spiritual crisis.

The poachers' secrets couldn't be kept forever. By the time Michael returned for his second go as a student, they'd all been scared off or drifted away from a campus that might be ripe for a new infestation. He came back with a scholarly confidence: from classroom to lecture hall, filing academic revelations in mental folders for random recall.

In the library, melding a philosopher's essay on laughter with his English instructor's edict—"All humor arises from switched context"—his eyes drifted up from the page to a woman on the opposite side of a long reading desk. Like him, too old for an undergraduate, she met his gaze, winked, and tossed her head backward, sending a fan of raven hair in a shimmering, iridescent arc over her shoulder. She was combing it out with spread fingers as she turned back to the video screen in front of her.

Licensed by the winking eye, he penciled a note, walked it around the desk, and placed it beside her: "Studying until six. Join me for dinner in town? Michael." He was hardly seated again before a return note came flying over the green lamps between them: "Sure. Starblanket."

In coed uniform of the season, a man's white dress shirt, faded jeans, and cloth-topped flat shoes, the striking dark-skinned woman wore no makeup around eyes old enough for faint laugh lines, reassuring signs of maturity. Each stolen glance at her brought a spark of pleasure, a conceit of her imagined complaisance. His rash invitation and her hasty reply left him reading passages twice, sometimes three times, with little comprehension. Bergson could as well have been the author of a comic book. An hour passed, with the hands of the library clock moving unconscionably slowly.

There was time to think more clearly. Starblanket? An aging hippie here in Jefferson's academy for Virginia's homegrown gentry? Switched context, and the joke on him? Her swift acquiescence far too easy. Now she seemed to be working the room, glancing here and there, ignoring him. Still sitting across the desk when he got up to leave, she followed him out of the library.

Michael was ready for combat, but she took his hand in hers as they walked toward the street, heading for the undergraduates' default café.

Was Starblanket a name she chose for herself?

"If it helps, I have a brother named Catwinkle. Call me Star."

"Your parents were the hippies?"

"There before the word."

Glancing to the side, he caught the full beauty of the woman walking beside him, her posture so erect, she might have been carrying a basket on her head. The coloring of her radiant face, maybe a mix from Africa and Asia, a mystery, to be probed with care.

In the restaurant she pulled him toward a rear booth. They ordered hamburgers and wine spritzers. He was pleased by her simple enthusiasm for the food, but her order of a second drink before the first was finished gave him a turn. He pulled his student card from his wallet, as if an exchange of credentials could be a social grace.

Insecure? Would he settle for her driver's license? When she opened her own wallet, he saw a cascade of credit cards fall in a plastic chain to the table. Starblanket Cole of Carlin, Virginia. Like Michael, she was twenty-four, with lost years to explain.

"You should relax," she said.

His shoulders fell. He moved his hands across the table toward hers.

"Not with me," she said. "I mean inhale the wide wind of this place. Hang out with some medical students, sit down with a math or law professor. Jump the artificial fences." It seemed she was already familiar with his year of caution, his hurried pace between classes, his grinding in the library. He explained he was on probation, his marks reviewed by the dean.

Was he still living at home?

"Not still," he told her. "Again."

Sucking the thumb that stirred her spritzer, she leaned closer, her eyes full on his. "I could show you the way to independence," she said. She was scribbling something on her paper place mat. Once finished with her food, she had to run. "My treat," she insisted, pulling out the plastic again, showing him all the ways she could pay.

He sat there for a few moments, thinking of the fool he'd been. He grabbed her place mat to see the "exciting figures" she'd left for him. Not numbers, but a few simple pencil lines with smudging for shadow, a bold portrait of his face with open, overeager mouth, a disarming likeness.

Walking back to his dormitory, he went out of his way to cross the Lawn between colonnade columns, sentinels of academic order, the architectural soul of the university—his stroll of scholarly purpose when discouraged. Whatever she wanted, the beautiful woman who had fled so abruptly, it wasn't him. If nothing else, he'd cadged a free meal; he'd be embarrassed if their paths crossed again.

But a few days later, leaving the cafeteria, she came from behind, tapping his shoulder, with something to tell him. She took his hand in that same commanding way and led him up to the Lawn, where they sat on the grass and she began to explain herself.

Not a full student, but a walk-on in a History of Film class. The instructor had arranged a seat for her. She was working her way through all the Lucys in the library's television archive, hired as a researcher for a book about Lucille Ball, proving that a prejudice against television had kept her off Chaplin's pedestal.

It was convincing up to a point. But some author's drudge? This elegance in coed garb with face and figure perfect to a fault. He imagined her on some swell's arm, wrapped in shimmering silk, glowing in diamond earrings. She lay back on the grass.

"You're as old as I am," she said, "so get it on."

He touched her cheek with a blade of grass. She flicked it away.

"Not you, your story. What happened to you?"

"You have to remember," he began, "in those days a lot of people were ingesting funny stuff, looking for their hidden selves. Hollow-eyed with pot." "Groggy with orgasm" left unsaid. Blowing past William Blake with the help of acid, they actually could see the world in a grain of sand.

Six of them dropped out together, packed into a crippled vintage station wagon, heading for California, throwing the

I Ching too often to be led in a straight line; San Francisco by way of New Orleans and Santa Fe, attracting a couple of fellow travelers along the way. His goddess Nadine snuggled next to him, assuring him the little canister of cannabis seed tucked behind the overhead cabin light would never be discovered by police.

Star rose on her elbows, new energy in her curiosity.

THE PLOT THEY SETTLED ON was an abandoned gold claim. Michael found work planting shrubbery for a nursery. He stayed long enough to claim unemployment compensation for a bad back, then worked in the commune as the gardener.

In their second California winter, they were full of sickness, stomach flu and high fevers. They heard vibrations rising from the mine shaft on barely audible frequencies, voices sounding like their names as they listened to nature for advice.

"I was too sick to move. Nadine looked for contradictions in my life." Why the vanity of hair to his shoulders? "I let her shave my head. She threw the hair into the compost, and the next week I was taking nourishment, on my feet again." Credit to the shorn vanity while he nursed Nadine through the same deathly flu.

By the end of winter, all of them were bald, and much distrusted in the area.

Starblanket lay back on the grass again. "You couldn't blame people," she said. "There were a lot of suspicious men roaming the land, looking for disciples."

That spring, he said, they found his hair woven neatly

into a bird's nest in a manzanita bush beside their garden, admiring the cunning weave.

"You think I'm making this up."

"Go on."

But it was Starblanket's turn.

HER FATHER, FROM SENEGAL, progenitor of height and posture; mother from Palestine, gifting fine Semitic chiseling and skin that turned brown to copper across her cheek. They met in high school in Shaker Heights. Honor students, they went on together to St. John's College, where Great Books pointed them toward social disaffection. They were leaders of a commune of other educated dropouts in an abandoned boardinghouse over the Shenandoah River, where Star was born in a bathtub of warm water.

Her raising, a difficult communal chore. Her parents believed her behavior was the sign of appropriate freedom. Others thought it needed stern correction. By the time she was six and riding a bus to the public school, she knew there was something twisted in her communal tutelage. She could remember house meetings at which the Starblanket problem led the agenda.

THEY WERE BOTH SITTING UP NOW, laughing at each other's preposterous stories, their stumble through that decade of impoverished purification, the era when girls became "ladies," people became "folks," theft became "liberation," and the only possible future would arrive "after the revolution." Star arriving in her commune at birth; he seduced into his by a child siren of countercultural magic. Both of them, safely on the other side, both shot through with cult antibodies, and ready to prove it.

That evening, she took him for a ride in a red convertible fresh from Detroit. She put the top down and made a loop around the campus while he sat beside her, explaining that living with his parents was only temporary. He'd worked the previous summer, making enough money as a night courier to cover room, board, and tuition for a whole year. He was trained to shoot a pistol worn in a shoulder holster. No, he couldn't tell her what he'd carried between cities because he wasn't told.

Did he have a little nest egg? "No? I can see you don't want to talk about money. I'll put the top down, and you can tell me more about Big Oak Flats."

"I don't mind talking about money," he said.

"Maybe later."

She had spun out of the university's orbit, driving uphill toward Monticello. "Jefferson," she said, "odd that such a smart guy died in debt. Did you know he came up with the coinage divisions and the decimal base for our money?"

Already he regretted lying to her. He confessed he'd never carried a pistol and his summer cargo was no secret, just canisters of feature films he moved between cities for a theater chain. He did have nine hundred dollars put aside for next year. He was thinking how foolish his fantasy of her favor. So beautifully proud in her lovely skin that diminished his pale imitation. And so appropriately in the driver's seat.

She turned the car into a scenic overlook where two other couples were already parked. "Relax," she said, placing her hand on his. "I'll put the top back up. What made you leave Big Oak Flats?"

"Aren't you the child of a purification camp?" he asked. "Why do all communes disintegrate—shifting alliance, doctrinal dispute, the odious introduction of a work schedule, shirked duties, the monotony of a small connubium."

"Whoa!"

"There were only a few of you, right?"

She sat back, as if recalculating. "No," she said. "Base Metals wouldn't be right for you. Maybe too risky."

He was recalculating, too. The truth was his "lady" Nadine had taken up with one of the other "folks." He'd left California in search of a Mexican healer called Merco, with a reputation in herbs and mushrooms. After weeks of searching southward down a trail of communes much like his own, he found the medicine man in a dusty camp outside Renson, Nevada.

It was surprising how quickly he was invited into the wise man's hut. "You're suffering," Merco said. "Do you have a driver's license? Can you hunt rabbits? Keep a garden in the desert? Help the woman around the house?" Merco denied the report he had broken a man out of jail with a tornado.

The woman, Tess, was a big, brooding presence in the one-room hut, in no need of Michael's help in the cramped quarters. Dismissive at first, she took to him with fond attention as he strengthened, ladling extra portions of her rabbit stew into his bowl. In a stolen moment she might stroke his head, lamenting she had no child of her own to fondle, and stretching a confidence to Michael's embarrassment: "Merco is not strong, he can't make me finish." She didn't need to tell Michael this; he slept on a cot only a dozen feet away from the couple; her chronic disappointment, a naked, audible fact.

There was no quick remedy for Michael's melancholy. Herbs would only follow days of meditation. First orders were "Let your hair grow out" and "Don't bring your marijuana in here." His first job was hunting rabbits for the dinner pot with a .22 rifle. He soon became the Mexican's chauffeur and assistant. Before a healing, he would pass through the rooms of a house, swinging a coffee can of cedar coals, then fan the smoke out the front door with a feather, Merco following behind, whispering incantations. There was no medicine cabinet in the wise man's hut, only a jar holding a shriveled mushroom on the windowsill. A lot of trouble flew through the air unseen.

STAR WAS ROLLING HER EYES.

"Not at you," she said. It was the proliferation of healers in that age of aggressive wisdom—from Delhi to Dupont Circle, worldwide therapies—a bit of luck the two of them had survived without brain damage, or the permanent affect of superior morality.

"I'm a fraud, too," she confessed. "There's no man writing a book about Lucille Ball."

Her advantage melting, her bronzed elegance transmuting into something touchable. She was working for two men, one a stockbroker, the other an insurance underwriter—soliciting for them on the campus. They kept her in the red convertible, and were gradually making her rich. Did Michael know that a student opening a life policy today could be worth a quarter million at thirty? She pulled a pocket calculator out of her handbag to prove it, speaking an unfamiliar jargon—upside potential, downside risk, base metals again, over the counter, unlisted, or maybe a life policy.

"You have to have a little courage," she said, squeezing his hand.

Driving down the mountain, they made a plan to meet that week in the cafeteria.

But where did she live?

"In the neighborhood."

Her evasion revived suspicion. When she dropped him off at the edge of campus, his feet were firmly on the ground again as he detoured between the vigilant pillars of the colonnade on the way to his dormitory, in mind again of academic purpose and the dean.

When they met that week, her first words as she glanced around were "Look at all these kids, larking as if their contented futures are guaranteed, with no idea how they'll pay for them." As if she were sitting in a roomful of financial nincompoops. She asked for more about his adventure in the desert.

HE'D HEARD MERCO'S WOMAN telling the wise man that Perdue chickens were too expensive, that a skinny fryer could hold the spirits just as well. By then, all the smoke wafting and incantation might have been laughable except that Merco's patients got better. The woman said, "The boy doesn't know how to shop."

"Don't pay attention to her," Merco advised him. "She

can't make a child. It makes her ashamed. Do what she tells you."

Everything changed when Michael told him about his hair woven into a bird's nest in Big Oak Flats. Merco darkened. "That's hurting you," he said.

Finally, diagnostic certainty. "He was genuinely worried about me." As long as the nest survived, Michael could never move forward; the woven hair was turning him in circles. His life would keep repeating itself. "You have to find that nest and bring it to me."

The woman had grabbed Michael's arm as if she'd never let go. "You know the boy will never find it," she said.

"But I couldn't stay unless I did as Merco said. I hitched all the way back there and I did find it. Five hundred miles each way." The manzanita bush had suffered from drought, leaving the nest exposed as a single ornament, a little worse for weathering, otherwise intact.

Back on point: "Will I get stock certificates?"

"Better to keep them in the street names, Greenman and Raddler. The guys I live with."

THEIR FREQUENT MEETINGS that fall turned heads on the university paths, her bronze elegance, hand in hand with the thin man who looked like Daniel Day-Lewis. The black-haired pair, too old to be undergraduates, were a campus curiosity. From a distance you might have thought they were arguing, their exchanges so animated. Before Michael went home for Thanksgiving, he'd written a five-hundred-dollar check to Greenman & Raddler for a thousand shares of Base Metals, an Alaskan mining venture.

Star's market parlance had become part of his own hopeful vocabulary: upside potential and a likely split, his penny stock multiplying on news of a successful land claim. And the enticing name, Base Metals, with its overtone of financial alchemy that might transmute a modest investment into a retirement fund.

Now that she had his money, would she disappear? he dared to ask.

What! Did he think the prospect of his puny investment could buy her interest in him? She sped away in a pique, leaving him curbside. He faced his books with a new ferocity, won praise for a paper on Conrad, Wittgenstein, and the limits of language. He chose philosophy as his major, planning ahead for a thesis on thinkers outside the academic canon. Karl Kraus, for example, and the death of a culture's language by its romantic practitioners.

WHEN HE SAW STARBLANKET AGAIN, the forsythia was in bloom. His only contact with her had been her warm presence in a dream. He found her sitting on the upper tier of the campus's outdoor amphitheater, dressed like the businesswoman she'd pretended not to be, in black slacks and jacket.

"Working the town," she said. Messrs. Greenman and Raddler had threatened to cut her loose for wasting too much time with the thin man who looked like Daniel Day-Lewis. "You do, a little bit," she told him. She had come there hoping to see him.

What about his investment?

"The children of communes are apt to revolt. They make

an early pledge to middle-class membership," she said, as if her evasion could answer for the dollar figure he hoped for. She was explaining how her parents' contentment with a prosperous poverty had become an irritation to her; no one went hungry, but there was little ambition, no hustle. Most of the men, passable carpenters; the women worked at a nearby boarding school for troubled children.

Permutation in the group's couplings, hardly noticed as an infant, had been confusing to her as a six-year-old, embarrassing at twelve, and beyond tolerance as a teen. Her escape had been public school, where she excelled and grew scornful of the commune's short shelf of "great books," flanked by the *Whole Earth Catalog* and *Zen and the Art of Motorcycle Maintenance.*

Of course there had been pleasures. The men were outliers if they couldn't charm with a guitar and folk repertoire. But the group's relaxed presentation had become performance, an avoidance of the hurts and scars of intramural histories. Endless punning and banter, skirting sincere exchange. At the dining table, frequent audible quotation marks, or silence. If someone took too long answering a question, her father, interrupting, reprising academic anxiety: "Stop! Put your pencil down. Pass your blue book to the right." It was conversational prison, irony allowed.

After molding Star into shy obedience, the communards were hurt that their ward regarded them with baleful suspicion. Twenty-two mingling adults, all that pure communion, denying jealousies, with only one child to show for it, and they wondered at her sullen retreat. By fifteen, statuesque and stunning, she was vulnerable in that house of many bedrooms, where intimacy was an expectation. Her parents moved her off the mountain to a farm in the valley, where a school bus could pick her up and she'd do chores for bed and board.

In Nevada again with the nest, Merco had taken Michael farther into the desert for his purification ceremony. The area was smoked with sage. A fire of juniper branches was lit, and a chicken breast quarter placed on the ground. Merco stood behind Michael, brushing the air down into the chicken, which was then placed on the fire with two sticks.

The wise man took the nest and began to pull hairs from it, straightening them one at a time, and dropping them onto the fire. He had removed only a few when a stubborn strand pulled the nest apart and most of it fell to the ground, rolling off like tumbleweed, then breaking up in the stiff breeze, before they could catch it. Marco, despondent as he straightened the few remaining hairs, doubted it would be enough. Michael's life would keep doubling back on itself no matter the direction he took.

He wouldn't upset his guardian with doubts after all the earnest concern for his recovery.

After the nest mishap, there was no place for him in the wise man's hut, where Marco said he would only be waiting to be turned again. "When it happens, you won't even notice it."

Michael retreated all the way east to his parents' home in Northern Virginia, where they welcomed their prodigal without shaming. He could begin his life again with a letter of contrition to a new dean of admissions and preparation for a more mature assault on the university.

FRIDAY EVENINGS AFTER shakes and burgers, confessor and supplicant by turns, they faced each other in the front seat of the convertible. Who the greater sinner? The one who invested five hundred dollars not to lose sight of her, or the one who accepted his money as tribute? The question hung in the air as the pair, who'd never more than held hands, strayed further from their promises to Greenman, Raddler, and the dean, their pasts unfolding faster now, their mutual honesty a slow-working aphrodisiac.

AFTER HIGH SCHOOL, with the smell of the barnyard still on her clothes, Star would be packed off to Baltimore to live with Audrey, a childhood friend of her mother's from Shaker Heights, who lived singly in an apartment building where Star was in walking distance of her art college. On first glance at her friend's beautiful daughter, Audrey reneged. "This isn't going to work," she said, maybe imagining a procession of Star's young suitors hiding in her closets, but Star moved in, and after a summer of seclusion and silence in her bedroom, Audrey was more worried about Star's mental health than her competition. At the art college she won praise for drafting skills, but quickly learned that figurative storytelling held little interest for a faculty promoting performance art and colored abstraction.

Michael broke into her story with news that wouldn't wait. His philosophy professor had challenged the class:

How many times had they heard "That would be reinventing the wheel"? "Write a paragraph on this tired nonsense." Michael wrote, "No one invented the wheel. Anyone could see a round rock would roll downhill. The invention was the axle."

"Yes!" He was told to read his answer aloud to a full auditorium.

His small triumph did little to slow Star's narrative, first a trickle, then a waterfall.

While she pondered a penniless future in the creation of unwanted likenesses, her parents' commune was splitting in a dozen directions. They moved off their mountain retreat to a house on Capitol Hill in Washington, finding jobs in the president's war on poverty. It seemed shameful to tell their daughter there was a lot of money in poverty, but already they were on a track to the middle class.

In her final year of art college, Star had her own moment of fame. A critic at the city's paper picked her work as best in the show of the graduating class. "More satisfying design," he wrote, "in one corner of Ms. Cole's sensitive, life-affirming representation than all the splashed abstraction on the walls around it."

The young critic, Moishe Kline, a jazzed-up brain topped with a wild field of red hair, came looking for her in the college cafeteria and found her at a table, alone. He got right down to it—the damage being done at American art academies, disregard for the representation of felt life, the facile worship of design. He said he'd like to use Star's work to illustrate a book on the loss of a nation's latent talent. It would require some time together.

WHEN SHE TOLD HER PARENTS a friend was driving her over to visit them in Washington, it was a first. Hoping not to embarrass her and presuming nature's protocol as practiced on the commune, they made up only one extra bed. They'd guessed wrong, and scurried to lay sheets and a blanket on the sofa. Though presuming intimacy, her mother was actually concerned with Star's abrupt new interest in any man. At dinner he'd hardly gotten a spoon into his soup when she attacked.

"Moishe, what do you think are the three most important books ever written?"

Star spoke before the crimson line on Moishe's neck could climb to his chin. "If your commune's bookshelf was any guide, there were only two—*Zen and the Art of Motorcycle Maintenance* and the *Whole Earth Catalog*." Not ready to let her mother abuse the man who recognized her value, sight unseen.

"But Star," Moishe said, "I saw you the first time I visited the campus. After that I couldn't stay away." More fool he.

The next day he drove home alone, and she, disenchanted, took the train back to Baltimore.

In the following weeks she fell into a depression disrupting sleep and appetite. Contemplating self-destruction, she accepted help. Paxil and its calming cousins were in fashion for deep distress, but her anxiety had no respect for chemical repair. Failed titrations of the pills gave way to head-on adoption of a therapist's advice. "Get comfortable in your own skin. You need to practice letting others admire you."

After a single visit to the faculty lounge, she was hired to sit as a model for the art college's drawing students, where she gradually learned to accept their excited observation as her therapy. Eventually she sat naked and at ease on the school's life-class stools.

The therapist who brought Star back from despair couldn't predict what would come out the other side. But with twice-daily nude presentations of herself, she made a sustaining wage, enough to ease into the day in a coffee shop with a sketch pad in her lap.

Here Messrs. Greenman and Raddler entered her life. The pair of nicely groomed men sat to her advantage one morning, comparing manicures over the financial page spread between them.

"She's cut my nails spatulate. My cuticles are sore."

Star took up her charcoal for a visual record of the conversation. Before she'd finished her sketch, the men's dwindling business prospects in Baltimore, the desertion of their sales assistant, harassment by a federal agent, and their coming removal to Charlottesville were all incorporated in her sketch of the pout and smirk of these stock and life insurance salesmen. Amused and sympathetic, she fell into conversation with them. They bought her drawing for fifty dollars and became her morning coffee pals.

A month later, she moved with them to Charlottesville, lured by the new car, an extraordinary salary, and lodging. The men's rooms on the second floor of their new home had a connecting bathroom, where the sound of doors swinging freely between them each night assured her easy sleep in her room on the floor below.

"GET IN," STAR SAID. "Here," she continued, returning his investment, handing him five hundred-dollar bills. "It's time you started paying for gas."

She drove halfway around the campus before turning north on Route 29. Something different. Fine with him. They were crossing the Rivianna bridge when she asked, "Did you bring your toothbrush?" and he woke fully to his gentle kidnapping. He wouldn't make a fool of himself by answering.

The landmark at the point of no return between Charlottesville and Washington was a roadside barn hung with used bicycles and tricycles and a yard full of the same, remembered this trip as the point where Starblanket spoke again: "Never mind, you can share mine."

Michael could have been floating into next week on a ship, at the mercy of the helm. But he was in the red car, only the eddying air around it looking backward. Beyond the reach now of the dean's frown and the disappointed sentinels of the colonnade. The highway stretched ahead in a perfectly straight line toward her parents' home on Capitol Hill.

Michael was not speechless—that is, he had a speech or perhaps Socratic dialogue in mind that touched on morality, but no inclination to raise debate that led back to his willful gullibility. He did ask about the car; wouldn't they try to reclaim it? They wouldn't dare go to court, she said. "It's ours."

Speaking into the silence of his overwhelmed imagination, she explained Raddler was the one who had a score to settle, taking compensation from an unfriendly world; the one who invented Base Metals. Unaware of her planned escape, he'd given her a new ghost stock, Prospectiva, to peddle to the young folk of the university, the same who recoiled at his plimsolls and pastel polos.

As they crossed a final bridge, the grandeur of the Capitol dome was lost in contemplation of his "willing suspension of disbelief," that trope of his professors snapping at his conscience—denial of all the likely outcomes of this unlikely journey.

"Ready for the pop quiz?" Star asked.

At dinner that night, he was describing the first of the three most important books, just getting to the compromise intended in *Critique of Pure Reason* when Star's mother, outfaced, turned the conversation to Star's progress at Greenman & Raddler, then shifted to the failure of the dessert she'd made, guiding him away from any further answers to her favorite examination.

After the meal, her father brought out folders of Star's early drawings made at the mountain commune. There was much bemused reminiscence of communal life as practiced in Virginia and California before it was time for bed. Star must have warned her mother about the visit, because the guest room was arranged with options. Made-up beds along opposite walls, with a four-part screen that could be unfolded between them.

Star had meant it about the toothbrush, handing it to him when she was finished at the sink. "So, I guess we've already kissed by proxy," he said as they sat on one of the beds and helped each other undress. She had packed a nightgown but didn't take it out of the bag. He watched as she pulled sheet and blanket over her, then walked naked over their scattered clothes and got into the bed on the other side of the room.

They lay in silence for a while before she said, "Are you going to stay over there all night?"

"Yes," he said.

There were a few minutes of silence before he asked if her parents had stuff to make waffles with.

Probably, she thought.

"Maybe we'll just have scrambled eggs," he said.

THE NEXT MORNING AFTER BREAKFAST, Star took the passenger seat and Michael drove them to Berkeley Springs, where they took a room in the hotel, hiked up to an Appalachian ridge, and came back for a soak in the family hot tub. At dinner they spoke softly of the spells they were leaving behind, the doomed wisdom of communes, the siren call of scholarship, the alchemy of the stock market.

They washed his underwear for tomorrow. Return trips to Charlottesville for their things and a final destination were nuisances tossed aside like their clothes. Later their noisy tangle brought a grin to the clerk at the night desk below. In the sweet musk of his satiety, Michael supposed his life lay in a straight line ahead of him, his for the taking.

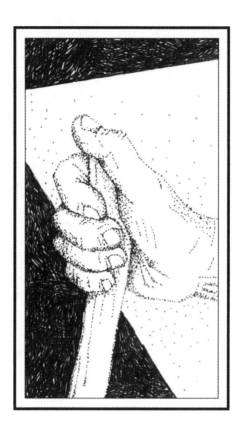

*A balanced pivot on the walking stick put him
on a downhill stretch.*

SURVIVAL

LESTER SNUFFLED UP a handful of pills, washed them down with some water, considered the wrinkles in his morning mirror, and took a second gulp to get the fat oval one past his tonsils. His clothes were wrinkled, too, and who cared—the T-shirt and briefs he slept in, the soiled trousers he pulled on, the cracked boots he laced while sitting on the end of the bed without waking her. At the stairway he got a firm grip on the railing because the big oval one working with the heart pill could throw him off-balance if he moved too quickly.

Years ago, Lester had been farrier to Mr. Mellon's barns at the training track, putting racing plates on young thoroughbreds that might pull a nail into his thigh right through his chaps for no reason whatever. Other farriers let him have most of the work at the track. He made a living at it, plus galloping Mr. Mellon's horses when he was still skinny and fearless.

Lester gave up the galloping at forty-five, when belly spilled over buckle. He had thirty more serviceable years before the heart troubles came on. That, and the many thousand horses that had leaned on him, put him out to pasture. He was on the heart pills now. One of them cost more than a year's groceries, so a much cheaper one came to him now from Turkey by way of Canada. Reading the list of side effects, you might wonder he was standing at all.

Steady at the back door, he took his walking stick, and was off down the driveway. Miriam would be watching from the window. Once on the graveled road, he took no notice of her calling to put his mask on, hoping he could get past Graham's place at the corner without being seen by Graham, Sir Talks-A-Lot, who flew the rebel flag, and claimed a score of listeners to his podcast about his right to display the banner. Graham, a Britisher.

A balanced pivot on the walking stick put Lester on a downhill stretch, one foot carefully in front of the other, but Graham's wife came out her back door to catch him beside her garden. Her head was lowered as she hurried forward, arm raised, waving a finger to stop him. "I heard they put a dead coon in your driveway," she called. "That's a shame. That one and his woman gone near four years."

Lester stared at her, holding his balance on the hill. Jerry Stack used to live in the Grahams' place. People called Stack a jackleg out of jealousy; he could do most anything for you, even put an addition on your house and top it with a standing seam roof bent with his own roofing irons. Then charge so little, you'd worry for his hard-pressed wife. Graham's wife was still going on about the last president's family, how they kept church and a tight rein on the two girls. "Anyway, a settle-aged man like you shouldn't have to put up with that. . . . Say, you're one who'd be interested in this. . . ."

"Interested?"

"Well," she said, "you had his signs up in your yard, didn't you? It's no secret you . . ."

Lester took her moment of hesitation to turn, gather balance, and continue his drift down the hill.

"I can tell you where the COVID comes from," she called after him. "It's not the bats." Her ready science came from her receptionist job at the veterinary clinic. "It's from the Chinese laboratory," she called. And she wouldn't be getting the vaccination, because "that's coming from China, too."

Her voice trailed off as a house built into the hillside came into view where the Ramparts used to live, Pete and Patricia, who sang hymns on their porch in the evenings. O'er the Ramparts we watched, he mused, thinking how years ago he had walked by here with the minister's son, who confided, "They got a baby up in there," as if a crime were in progress. True, there was a baby, an embarrassment to Patricia's niece, sent to Worton until her shame passed over her hometown. Pete lost his meat-cutter job at Safeway, caught stealing steaks one night. He and Patricia moved away and a commuter to the city and his wife moved in and took up with the foxhunting people in Middleburg.

For Lester, who had lived in Worton all his life, any of four ways from the village crossroad was a stroll down memory lane. At eighty-one, content in his achievement of daily labor, he'd lived at no other's expense from birth, comfortable in the old cottage where he'd been all his life. He imagined eternity's favor for a man like himself, who wanted so little, expecting no more than he earned. His nearest neighbors vied for his attention; on one side a man who discharged a heavy pistol every day at a human silhouette; on the other, a family whose yard sign announced THIS HOUSE WELCOMES ALL. He moved slowly, but not as a stranger, familiar with a tale of each freehold he passed, the knots that bound clans and interlopers, come and gone on the Worton landscape.

He stopped a moment, letting some dizziness pass. Faltering forward, he swayed on the loose gravel as he passed the white stucco bungalow where the bank manager, Millard, had lived. Millard, who had a stone ax head and forty-two arrowheads in his basement, all found the same afternoon on an island in the Potomac after the 1949 flood. He used to give cuttings from his holly tree to every house in Worton at Christmastime. When Lester was eleven, Millard's granddaughter had pulled him into the basement there to see his Indian museum, but when they were down there, she got in front of him and told him to touch her wherever he wanted. At that age, he wasn't up to the job. Millard's place had passed on to a grandson, who taunted the homosexual who lived at the top of the next hill whenever he went by on his saddle horse.

Don't let the old man in, Lester thought to himself as he willed himself along a furlong of flat. He couldn't help it if every house he passed had such a grip on his memory. Every one of them had belonged to someone who'd left the village or passed away. He'd come back right after his army service, settling into the same stone house his father had bought for a song in the Depression. Maybe the oldest house in the village, old beyond any record of its building—a square block of two-foot-thick stone walls, with a shed-roof section added by his father to accommodate twentieth-century plumbing: a kitchen sink and a toilet.

Any embarrassment of inheritance offset by the house's age and condition—the thick walls chinked with a mortar mixed with horsehair, and covered with white milk paint, later plastered with a nineteenth-century formula of white cement and lime to hold it all together when the chinking began to crumble. The original roof of rough-hewn chestnut rafters, pine boards, and cedar shingles was still there under metal painted black and tarred again and again over the years, treating leaks that ran in secret channels between the multiple layers. Lester's parents left this puzzle of shelter and upkeep to him, moving to a tract in North Carolina, where their last years were blissed with a vacuum system that ran through the walls, a garbage pit in the sink, and a machine that dried dishes after washing them.

The old cottage had a lost early history, no county record of the property before the mid-eighteenth century, when Loudoun County was split off from the Fairfax grant. When he was in grade school, a man driving through Worton told Lester he used to visit here in summers and the week he came there was always a circus across the road, with a lion that roared all night. In those days the village had three stores and a blacksmith, and whipped Leesburg in the county baseball league. The visitor remembered the flat stone set in the ground by the front steps, still there, with CARTER crudely chiseled into it.

BACK HOME AFTER THE ARMY, Lester corresponded with a "university without walls." They gave him a certificate in the humanities, but he settled on horses' feet, and got himself known in Mr. Mellon's barn at the training track. Mr. Mellon took a shine to him and gave him a retainer and friendship worth more than the Christmas turkey—even a ride one time on his jet plane to the Saratoga yearling sale.

Miriam wouldn't get on the plane and so missed the Saudi who floated into the room in a white robe and held his cigarette between his third and fourth fingers and outbid Mr. Mellon for a colt that won the Preakness.

In Worton all his life, most of it with Miriam, who came along right after Kate. Don't let the old man in, he reminded himself, but memory rode roughshod over the intention. Kate stuck there for a time as he ambled, unsteady, along the flat; Kate, who had knocked on his door, eager for friendship. More than eager for several months, then leaving him miserable, missing bedroom behavior he hadn't thought of before or would ever know again. She left him for a boy who was grazing on the community college campus where she was studying to be a physical therapist. "You don't flex a muscle," she'd taught Lester, "flexion is a skeletal process." Maybe the newly acquired knowledge had something to do with what he hadn't given her. She must have really liked the other boy, because, first thing, he gave her the clap and, little bothered, she skipped off with him to Canada, beyond reach of his draft board.

Miriam came next and forever. He was relieved to be thinking of her, needing her support to push him up the hill in front of him, hoping he could make it to the top without the pain coming into his arm.

Miriam had come to the village, bicycling down Worton Road from the west, stopping at the corner to ask the way to the apiary, where she'd gotten a job for the summer. "You passed it back by the church," Lester had explained, holding her in conversation long enough to explain Worton's lack of rental opportunity, which wasn't going to matter, as things fell out.

She might have entered his life humming "You can't always get what you want," offering instead something he needed, weaning him from Kate's enchantment with a less practiced behavior, neither animal nor missionary. She had a wit that jumbled things, making him wonder at the zany brain he was sleeping with.

She'd rise with him at 5:00 A.M. to watch early galloping at the track, suggesting one day that horses should be trained in the opposite direction around the oval, as if they could be wound up like a spring, primed with a new energy when set in the right direction, the more eager to make left turns. Mr. Mellon got a chuckle out of that. He said they should have tried it on Jay's Farthing, the Saratoga colt that had been such a disappointment. Such notions gave Lester doubts, wondering if Miriam's was a wry wit performed, or spontaneous innocence. Soon enough all doubt shifted to fear she might leave him. He relaxed when she began to call him "Toots" and fussed for a regular change of his underwear.

He was humming "Don't let the old man in" again, moving slower as he passed the pond where young hellions used to do their mud bogging, roaring into the water, covering their shiny trucks with green slime and flying mud before silence settled back on the hills. He remembered the quiet cursing while a winch pulled all that vanity out of the mire, and wondered where that decade's wastrel energy had gotten to. At their age, he'd come out of the county high school and done his army service. They taught him Morse code and sent him to England, where he hammered dots and dashes into five-letter code groups on a heavy typewriter.

He trilled his tongue over nine dots followed by a "dah"—s h i t—faster than he could put one foot in front of the other, because the Beale boy's pickup truck was raising a dust cloud as it approached him. It came straight at him for a pranking moment, leaving Lester staggering backward against the bank. As it passed, he saw a girl sitting beside Beale, laughing as she punched his shoulder, and two metal balls swinging under the truck's rear bumper.

Lester got himself back on the road without falling, moving forward again, toward the glass-front house with guy wires strung overhead, tying a tall radio antenna to three corners of the property. A cellist for the county symphony operated a shortwave radio in there. He'd assured Lester the gear and tackle were worth the expense. The year before, he said, he'd saved an African's life, relaying a doctor's directions from Boston to Ghana.

But his house was still known as "the scholars' place," for the couple who had moved there before him. They had come through the village, introducing themselves as "Ph.D. candidates, both of us." Miriam told them her husband, Lester, had been to the "university of four walls." Not so far off the mark, considering all the months he'd spent shut in his attic room with his textbooks.

Beside him on the road had been stone walls most of the way, walls that surrounded former farm fields on this side of the county two hundred years ago, many tumbled, frost-heaved and root-spilled, some still intact, hidden behind grapevine, honeysuckle, arm-thick poison ivy climbing the locust trunks beside the invading ailanthus and sumac; the oldest walls built by the farmers themselves. He felt a pride of place walking this road; of all the houses he passed, none of their occupants had been here longer than he.

Now he was passing a wall so exact in level and plumb, it might have been laid on the landscape by a fussy geometer. The new house behind it had a complex of angles and dormers to drive a roofer crazy. It was the home of the architect who'd designed it, a man who said the village was built so long ago, you could excuse some houses for their lack of imagination, busy as those people must have been with survival, their hand-dug wells, the garbage and outhouse pits, the fieldwork, no time for niceties. Come winter, no one came around to plow the architect's driveway.

Lester's destination was the Pastor Hill Cemetery, graveyard to Battle Grove Baptist, where Black dead lay under a motley of rough stone and more recent polished marble. There he could rest before his amble home. Charles, who had galloped with Lester at the training track, had drowned in the pond behind the Millard place, and was buried at Pastor Hill. And a girl shot in the university massacre in Blacksburg was there under ground not yet grassed over.

It was a quarter hour before the cemetery came into view. He was annoyed to see someone there, a Black man bending over, mending the graveyard wall. It would be rude to sit while he worked. Lester was ready to turn back, but the man stood up from his work and raised a beckoning hand. Not to offend, Lester came slowly forward.

The road ran next to the cemetery, and in a few minutes the two men were next to each other, on opposite sides of the wall. "Mister Lester," he said, "you best sit."

Lester had no choice. He collapsed onto the wall beside the fallen section.

The old Black man had short white hair, cheeks sunken into toothless gums, and his own infirmity, a palsied hand that shook when he put down the stone he held.

"Do I know you? From around here?" Lester asked him.

"Over to Willisville."

"Do I know you?" he asked again.

Lester thought if he sat to rest for a while, he'd be ready to walk home. If he got the shaky old fella talking, it might seem less an intrusion. The man picked up another stone and stood looking at it. "You was the one swimming with Charles," he said. "He lies over there."

Lester winced. Should he let it pass, or try to explain how there was nothing he could have done?

"This is my uncle lying here." The old man pointed down at the grave next to his work.

"Well, that's some coincidence."

"He taught me how to do this. I was young, going nowhere. He put me opposite and said, 'You do ever' thing on your side I do on mine.' You live in Miz Johnson's house."

Lester, swallowing something sour, had to explain. "No, my father bought it from Louise Grant. I could tell you a story." How many times had he told it? It was stale, no humor left in it, only a little shame in recounting another's hardship. "They had her septic tank turned backward, so the sewage backed up in her toilet. She threw her hands up and gave up. That's when my father bought it. It was in the Depression."

The old man found the right spot for a stone, and stood up to face Lester. "Yes, suh, and Miz Grant got the house at sheriff's auction when Miz Johnson was pushed out for the taxes."

"I never found any record of that."

"There's tongues for telling it. It was Judge Carter gave the house to the Johnsons at the Freedom. The house and acre it sit on."

He reached down for another stone. "Um-huhn," he continued, talking to himself, "Miz Johnson's great-great-grandson got taken into the magnet school. So, now who's smart?"

Lester had tipped forward, hearing his own walls pulled so abruptly from honorable acquisition, his long unchallenged tenure in the village. He tried to get up, but his legs wouldn't work. The sour taste rose again in his throat. He swallowed, but it rose again and surged. He turned on the wall and vomited a yellow drizzle of his morning pills into the graveyard. He heaved again, but nothing came.

"Put your head 'tween your legs, Mister Lester. I got the anywhere phone."

"No, goddamn it! Don't call anyone."

The old man began murmuring a prayer.

Lester, struck dumb with shame, wondered if he was getting the scythe man's signal. He tried moving his legs again but got no response.

"I'll be all right," he said.

The Black man stood silent, watching, then bent down to his work again.

"I suppose winter's hard on a wall," Lester ventured.

"Wasn't winter did this," the man said aloud.

Lester waited for him to explain. Instead, the man asked, "You still got a pot on the floor for the drip?"

Lester winced again.

"Willie, did the tarring for you this year, say you got a pot on the kitchen floor for the rain."

He went back to fitting a stone.

"There's no drip," Lester said.

The old man's gentle insult was maybe a signal for him to leave. He would have obliged if he could, but it was a job just holding himself steady while seated. He watched the man's shaking hand, and considered their mutual decay.

"I'll be fine," he said.

"Do your missus know which way you went?"

"I said I'll be fine."

"Why don't you go on where you need to be? Why you watching this?"

"You've got an eye for it, don't you?"

The old man tried a stone and set it aside. "Turn it three ways, still won't go, no use persisting. No bad stone. Ever' one got a home somewhere down the line. It stay put 'less someone knock it off."

He worked on for a while in silence with Lester sitting only a few yards away, in spell to the progress of the wall. The stonework continued methodically for another hour. Finished, the old man stood, wiped his hands on his overalls, and turned to Lester. They watched each other, Lester wondering why the old fella wouldn't just leave. He couldn't stare him down, didn't even know he was trying to.

The man began to explain how he was kin, two generations off, from one of Mr. Mellon's grooms who had worked with Lester, and how his wife's family was related to the drowned boy Charles. He pointed to where tire tracks ran right next to the wall, evidence of the grave-yard's latter-day antagonists.

"Mister Lester," he said, "you ever think to put a porch back on the house the way it used to be?"

He couldn't think what to say.

"I wonder is the attic still split in two rooms? Is the stair to it fixed?"

The old man might have been the caretaker of the house, the way the list of particulars went on, or a county building inspector going through a checklist.

"I told you I got the anywhere phone."

"No!" Lester shouted at him.

It was noon before Miriam showed up in the car. Her hands flew up from the steering wheel when she saw him. "Didn't you think I'd be worried?" she called through the window. "You've been talking all this time?"

The old man took one arm, and Miriam the other, help-ing Lester into the car. Back behind the wheel, she leaned across her husband and said, "He didn't eat any breakfast. He didn't tell me where he was going."

The Black man nodded, touching the brim of a cap that wasn't there.

"Look to me like the heart dropsy," he said.

On the way home Lester couldn't make her understand.

"Of course he couldn't leave you like that," she said. "If they found you lying on the ground out here, he'd be the first one they'd come looking for."

"He knows every room in our house," Lester explained, "like he lived in it."

"Relax," she said. "You'll make yourself sick again."

"He had a sniff of the drain field. He stuck his nose

down our well. He knows about our problem with the county health."

Miriam was driving slowly to calm him, to let him see how far his foolish walk had taken him. Her creeping speed was an agitation. Seen from the direction of the Black graveyard, the houses he'd walked by had been thrown into a jumbled past. With nothing for it, he sat back in surrender to the old Black man he'd watched with fascination moving along the graveyard wall, his clear conscience on display, his shaking hand, persisting against a callous history, his satisfaction as each abused stone was returned to its natural home.

PREVIOUS PUBLICATION HISTORY

These stories appeared previously in the publications listed below.

"Tree Men": *Potomac Review*, Issue 74 (Spring 2024).

"North of Ordinary": *The American Scholar* (Spring 2007).

"Freak Corner": *One Story*, Issue 254 (June 2019).

"Their Grandfather's Clock": *Potomac Review*, Issue 71 (Fall 2022).

"Virgin Summer": *The American Scholar* (Summer 2011).

"The Voice of the Valley": *Oxford American*, Issue 58 (Fall 2007).

"Survival": *Country Zest & Style*, Vol. 5, Issues 5 & 6 (Fall 2023).

Bellevue Literary Press is devoted to publishing literary fiction and nonfiction at the intersection of the arts and sciences because we believe that science and the humanities are natural companions for understanding the human experience. We feature exceptional literature that explores the nature of consciousness, embodiment, and the underpinnings of the social contract. With each book we publish, our goal is to foster a rich, interdisciplinary dialogue that will forge new tools for thinking and engaging with the world.

To support our press and its mission, and for our full catalogue of published titles, please visit us at blpress.org.

Bellevue Literary Press
New York